FAULTLINE

THE RACHEL HATCH SERIES
BOOK 14

L.T. RYAN

with

BRIAN SHEA

For information contact:

contact@ltryan.com

http://LTRyan.com

https://www.facebook.com/JackNobleBooks

THE RACHEL HATCH SERIES

Drift

Downburst

Fever Burn

Smoke Signal

Firewalk

Whitewater

Aftershock

Whirlwind

Tsunami

Fastrope

Sidewinder

Redaction

Mirage

Faultline

Switchback

RACHEL HATCH SHORT STORIES

Fractured

Proving Ground

The Gauntlet

Ricochet

Join the LT Ryan reader family & receive a free copy of the Rachel Hatch story, Fractured. Click the link below to get started:

https://ltryan.com/rachel-hatch-newsletter-signup-1

ONE

THE HOOD'S THICK FABRIC STANK OF SWEAT AND chemicals, clinging to Ethan Voss's face like rotting gauze. He tried to breathe through his mouth, but his throat was raw—scraped hollow from screaming. Water. Too much water. His lungs still burned with phantom drowning, each breath shallow and panicked, fighting against the wet fabric that wanted to seal itself against his nostrils.

Three days ago, he'd been just another investigative journalist chasing shadows in the digital dark. Now, those shadows had teeth.

Carter's encrypted message had arrived. Voss had been hunched over his laptop in Busboys and Poets, the Georgetown coffee shop's late-night crowd providing perfect white noise for clandestine communications. The message was brief, clinical: "Have proof. AeroSight weaponized my research. Meet Sunday dawn, mile marker 47." But it was the attachment that had made Voss's blood run cold—satellite imagery of a farm in central California, overlaid with seismic data that showed stress patterns too precise, too localized to be natural. Three farmers dead. Their families told it was a freak geological event. The insurance companies had paid out without question.

Time had lost meaning in the dark. Could have been hours. Could have been days. His body told him it had been forever—muscles cramped into positions they were never meant to hold, joints grinding bone against bone with every micro-movement.

He'd spent forty-eight hours cross-referencing Carter's data with USGS reports, news archives, death certificates. The earthquake had lasted exactly eleven seconds. Magnitude 4.2—strong enough to collapse the old farmhouse, weak enough that seismologists barely noticed. But Carter's files showed something else: controlled frequency bursts, artificially induced stress fractures, a mountain taught to kill on command.

Rope cut into his wrists. Thick, coarse. Hemp maybe. The kind that leaves scars. His shoulders throbbed from being yanked back, arms bound to the chair behind him. His ankles, too—restrained, immobile. The bindings had been tied by someone who knew their craft. No slack. No give. Just steady, inexorable pressure that turned his hands into swollen, nerveless meat.

His body screamed, but in the dark, there was no one to hear.

Somewhere beyond the damp fabric covering his eyes, water lapped against wood. The Potomac, he guessed. That rhythm—lazy, patient, indifferent—he knew it. He'd written enough stories about corpses surfacing downstream to recognize the sound of death soaking through the planks. The river didn't care about your politics or your principles. It just waited, knowing that sooner or later, everything ended up in its current.

Just like the story he'd never get to write. The exposé that would have revealed how earthquake prevention had become earthquake creation. How AeroSight was field-testing a weapon that could topple governments while maintaining the perfect cover of a natural disaster.

Boot soles scraped across concrete. Two men, maybe three. Heavy footfalls, steady, deliberate. Not rushed. Not hesitant. Professional. These weren't street punks or wild-eyed fanatics. These were trained hands. Men who knew exactly how much the body could take before it folded. They'd been with him through the cycles—drowning and resurrection, drowning and resurrection—never speaking, just doing their work with the patience of craftsmen.

The boathouse reeked of age and neglect. Mildew. Motor oil. The copper taste of fear-sweat that had soaked into the floorboards from whoever had sat in this chair before him. Because there had been others, Voss was sure of that. This place had the feel of routine, of practiced efficiency.

How many other journalists had sat in this same chair? How many whistleblowers, government employees, inconvenient witnesses to inconvenient truths? The thought made his stomach clench with something beyond fear—the recognition that he was just the latest entry in a ledger written in blood and silence.

The door groaned open on rusted hinges. A gust of fresh air sliced through the stench of mold and fear. Light flooded the room—Voss could feel it warming the damp fabric of the hood. The quality of the silence changed. Someone new had arrived. Someone who made the professionals straighten their spines.

Footsteps approached. Slower now. More controlled. Different gait. Leather soles clicked with surgical rhythm across the concrete. Not boots. Dress shoes. Expensive ones. The walk of a man who'd never hurried anywhere in his life because the world waited for him, not the other way around.

A chair scraped across the floor—closer now. Close enough that Voss could hear breathing. Calm. Measured.

Voss could smell cologne. Subtle. Clean. European. The kind of scent that didn't announce itself so much as suggest status. It cut through the sour reek of his own body odor, a reminder that there were still people in the world who showered in the morning, who put on clean shirts, who lived in the light.

Then the hood was yanked away.

Light punched through his vision like a flashbang. He winced, eyes burning, tears streaking down his cheeks. For a moment, the world was nothing but white agony. Then, slowly, shapes emerged from the glare. A halogen work light balanced on a tripod in front of him. Concrete walls stained with water damage surrounded him. A figure in a chair, backlit like some corporate deity.

The blur resolved.

A man stood in front of him. Crisp dark suit, charcoal gray, tailored to perfection. Manicured hands rested on his hips. Hair precisely styled despite the humidity. Eyes cold as stone. He looked like he'd have been more at home in a Capitol Hill boardroom than a riverside torture room.

David Kern.

Voss's breath hitched. Not just from fear—he'd drowned in that already—but recognition. He'd seen Kern's face before: grainy surveillance shots, redacted dossiers, files passed from source to source like contraband. The ghost in the machine. The man who didn't exist except through whispers and wire transfers. But none of it captured the gravity of his presence. Kern didn't just command the room. He owned it.

"You're real," Voss croaked. "Didn't think you got your hands dirty."

Kern's expression didn't flicker. "Only when the cleanup's worth it."

He pulled a metal chair precisely three feet forward and sat, folding his hands on one knee. Everything about the movement was measured. Intentional. Controlled. This was a man who practiced sitting down until it became a weapon.

"I'm going to ask you a few questions, Mr. Voss," Kern said. His voice had a quality Voss had heard before in very expensive lawyers—calm, reasonable, and utterly without mercy. "I'd appreciate honest answers."

"Go to hell."

Kern smiled faintly, as if the insult was a weather report. "Eventually. But not today."

He leaned back, studying Voss like a biologist observing a wounded animal. Detached. Clinical. Those eyes took in everything—the tremor in Voss's hands, the way his left eye twitched, the rapid pulse visible in his neck.

"Who's your source?"

Voss forced himself to meet that gaze. It was like staring into an empty house—lights on, nobody home. Whatever made a person human had been excavated from David Kern long ago, leaving only purpose and efficiency.

"I don't know what you're talking about."

Kern's tone didn't change. "The whistleblower. The one feeding you information about AeroSight's special projects division."

"My job is exposing the truth," Voss said, the words coming out in a rush. Some part of him still believed in the speech, even here, even now. "That's it. Your company's been draining black-budget billions into programs that—"

"Spare me the manifesto." Kern cut him off without raising his voice. "You're not the first idealist to think you'd change the world with a blog post. Most of them are considerably less wet than you are right now."

A presence shifted behind Voss. He couldn't turn, but he could feel it—someone stepping forward. The torturer. The professional. Ready to go back to work.

"I've read your articles, Mr. Voss. All of them. You have a gift for turning speculation into scandal. But your last piece—the one about our guidance systems—contained information you couldn't have guessed. Technical specifications. Budget allocations. Things that exist only in classified databases."

Kern leaned forward. The movement was minimal yet somehow filled the space between them with threat.

"Last chance," he said. "The name."

"I told you," Voss said, forcing defiance into his voice even as his body shook. "I don't—"

The hood slammed down. The chair tipped. Then came the water.

Cold. Merciless. It surged into his nose, his throat, turning breath into liquid panic. His body convulsed against the ropes, muscles firing in ancient patterns of escape that went nowhere. Brain screaming. Thrashing. Dying. Dying. Dying.

Every instinct howled. Every cell in his body demanded air. The water was everywhere—in his lungs, his stomach, behind his eyes. He was drowning in the middle of a room, drowning while men watched, drowning because he'd thought the truth mattered more than survival.

They yanked him upright. Ripped the hood off.

Voss vomited water and bile, his body purging itself in great, wracking heaves. Air came in ragged gasps, each breath a miracle and a torment. Across from him, Kern hadn't moved. Still seated. Still calm. Watching with the patience of a man who had all the time in the world.

"The name."

Voss coughed, spat, wheezed. His resolve buckled under the weight of terror. He'd written about heroes, about people who died for their principles. But principles were just words when you were drowning. Just ideas that dissolved in water.

"Carter," he whispered. The name tasted like failure. "Samuel Carter."

Kern tilted his head, a subtle movement that somehow conveyed satisfaction without displaying it. "And what does Mr. Carter have for you?"

Voss's lips trembled. He was crying now, tears mixing with the water still dripping from his hair. "Files. Documents. About something called ... Rift. I don't know what it is. I swear I don't."

"When were you meeting him?"

"In two days. Diner off the Appalachian Trail. Near Front Royal."

"Where exactly?"

"You take the exit after mile marker forty-seven. Northbound side. Drive about five miles. The meet's at a place called Pete's Diner." The words spilled out like blood from a gut wound. "We're supposed to be meeting at dawn. 7AM."

"And how will he know it's you?"

"I told him to take a booth. Sit facing the door. I told him that I would come to him." Voss took a deep breath. "Plus, he's seen my headshot in the byline of my articles."

"What else?"

"That's everything. Please. That's all I know."

Kern absorbed this information without reaction. He stood, smoothing an invisible wrinkle from his jacket. The movement was unhurried, almost casual.

"You've been helpful, Mr. Voss. Let's talk about your future."

Hope sparked in Voss's chest—a desperate flicker in the dark. "You said you'd let me go."

"I said I wanted information," Kern replied. "I also said bad things would happen if you talked." He paused, letting the words sink in. "Past tense now. I'm afraid that window's closed."

Voss strained against the ropes, the hemp cutting deeper into already raw flesh. "Wait. Please. I have a daughter. She's—"

Kern cut him off with a glance. "No, you don't. You have two cats, a suspended license, and a drinking problem. Your ex-wife hasn't spoken to you in six months. She lives in Bethesda with her new husband—an accountant, I believe. Considerably more stable than a conspiracy theorist with delusions of Pulitzer grandeur."

The casual cruelty of it—the precise dismantling of his life in a few sentences—hit harder than the waterboarding. Kern knew everything. Had probably known it before Voss ever woke up in this chair.

He checked his watch. A Patek Philippe. Of course. "You've been off the grid for three days. Your editor thinks you're chasing a lead in Richmond. Your neighbor is feeding the cats. Mrs. Chen, apartment 4B. Sweet woman. Brings in your mail, too."

Kern stepped toward the door. "You wanted to expose the truth about AeroSight. Congratulations, Mr. Voss. You found it."

Voss thrashed his body against the chair, muscles straining against inevitability. "You can't do this! People will know—someone will—"

"No one knows," Kern said without turning back. "That was the point of choosing a river. The Potomac's kept secrets for two centuries. What's one more?"

A hand gripped the hood. Voss saw it coming this time—black fabric descending like a curtain on the final act.

"Please—"

The hood dropped. Darkness swallowed him whole.

He screamed—but the sound was weak, muffled, drowned by the thundering of his own pulse. The chair tipped again. Back, back, back, until the world inverted, and the water rushed in.

This time, the water didn't stop.

And then, nothing.

Kern's footsteps faded, measured and unhurried. The door creaked shut. The sound of expensive leather on concrete grew distant, then disappeared.

Somewhere beyond the black, beyond the drowning, the river kept lapping at the dock—lazy, indifferent, patient. It had swallowed revolutionaries and traitors, lovers, and liars. All of them ended up the same in its muddy embrace.

The Potomac always got what it wanted in the end.

TWO

TWENTY-ONE HOURS ON THE ROAD. FOUR HOURS OF FITFUL sleep on a motel mattress that smelled like defeat and cigarette smoke. Three states. Two gas station burritos she'd regret later. One thermos of black sludge that had the audacity to call itself coffee.

Hatch pulled the Jeep to a stop as dawn broke over Virginia, painting the sky the color of a fresh bruise. The parking lot was packed with eighteen-wheelers, their chrome grilles catching the early light like bared teeth. Diesel fumes mixed with the smell of bacon grease drifting from the diner's exhaust vent. Her stomach growled, reminding her that rage wasn't actually a food group.

The diner squatted beside the highway like it had grown there—a relic from when interstates had been new and progress meant linoleum floors and neon signs. The sign flickered: *Ro ky's 24 Hour*. The 'c' had given up years ago. Nobody seemed to mind.

Inside, the place was exactly what she'd expected. Chrome stools bolted to the floor in front of a counter that had seen better decades. Booths with cracked vinyl seats held together by duct tape and stubborn will. The smell hit her like a warm slap—bacon, coffee, fryer oil, and that brand of exhaustion that clung to places where people came to refuel between somewhere and nowhere.

A few truckers hunched over their plates, shoveling eggs into their mouths like they were stoking furnaces. One glanced up as she entered, his eyes catching on the scar that ran from her left ear to her jaw. His gaze lingered for a second—not hostile, just the idle curiosity of a man who'd seen plenty of hard miles himself—then dropped back to his hash browns.

Hatch picked a corner booth. Back to the wall, clear sight lines to both exits and the parking lot. Through the window, she could see her Jeep. The vinyl wheezed beneath her as she sat.

"You look like you wrestled a bear, honey."

The waitress materialized beside her table, coffee pot in hand like a loaded weapon. Her name tag read *Ginny* in faded letters. Somewhere north of sixty, with the kind of face that had smiled through recessions and heartbreaks and kept on serving eggs.

"Didn't win," Hatch said.

“Bears usually don't play fair.” Ginny poured coffee into the empty mug without any prompting. The stream was black as motor oil and probably twice as thick. "What'll it be?"

"Eggs over easy. And whatever the kitchen's best at that doesn't come frozen."

"That'd be the bacon. Cure it ourselves out back. Harry—that's the cook—his daddy taught him, and his daddy before that. Three generations of pig, right here in Virginia."

"Sounds like tradition."

"Or stubbornness. Hard to tell the difference sometimes." Ginny scribbled on her pad. "Hashbrowns?"

"Sure."

"Coming up."

Ginny headed back to the kitchen, orthopedic shoes squeaking against the linoleum. Hatch pulled out her phone—a flip model that belonged in a museum but couldn't be tracked worth a damn. She'd driven straight through from Texas, fueled by adrenaline and the kind of anger that burned clean and cold. The events in Riverton still played on a loop in her head. Power grids hijacked. A whole town held hostage. And the men responsible had vanished like smoke in the wind.

She dialed. The phone rang twice.

"For someone who left Talon, you sure like keeping tabs."

Ed Banyan's voice carried that particular mix of sarcasm and affection that came from a shared history of close calls and near-death experiences. Consistently there to give her a healthy dose of reality at every turn, and at this point in her life, probably the closest thing to a friend she'd let herself have.

"What can I say," Hatch said. "I have a hard time letting go."

"Or maybe you just can't help but step into a heap of shit everywhere you step."

"Huh, that's what that smell is."

After the incident in Riverton, Hatch had reached out to Banyan, tapping the extensive resources at his disposal. She hated doing it. As much as she liked Banyan, the thought of tying herself to the organization she'd parted ways with was less than desirable. Especially for someone who wanted to stay low and off the radar. But her code forced her hand, leaving her with no choice.

"Tell me you found something."

The pause on the other end killed any hint of levity. "I wish. Kern's clean. Harlan too. No fingerprints on Riverton, not even a smudge."

Hatch's jaw tightened. She stared out at the parking lot, watching a trucker check his load straps. "They caused a blackout, hijacked a town, and walked away without a trace. That's not clean. That's surgical."

"Preaching to the choir. But whoever scrubbed this knew what they were doing. Professional work. From the extent of my digging, you'd have thought I would be able to scrounge up something. I came up with nada. Zilch."

"What about Kern himself? Got a workup on his background?"

"Now that's where it gets interesting." She could hear Banyan shifting, probably pulling up files on one of his encrypted systems. "David Kern. On paper, he's a tech entrepreneur. Founded AeroSight Defense Systems eight years ago. But before that? Ghost. Rumors put him in

Syria, Yemen, Somalia. Private contractor work. The kind where governments need plausible deniability."

"Destabilization ops."

"Among other things. Word is he specialized in infrastructure warfare. Power grids, water systems, communications. Sound familiar?"

It did. Riverton had been a proof of concept. A demonstration. "And prior to all the private contract stuff? Wait, let me guess, ex-military?"

"Ding, ding, ding. You got it. But most of it's redacted. At a level I'm not able to access without raising some red flags. To put it bluntly, he's not someone you just walk up on," Banyan continued. "This isn't some corporate suit playing soldier. He's the real deal."

"Fine. Maybe I start with the mouthpiece. Harlan."

"The congressman?" Banyan's tone suggested he'd rather she announce plans to wrestle an actual bear. "Hatch, William Harlan sits on the House Intelligence Committee. He's got extremely high visibility, and he'll likely have a security team. And don't forget lawyers."

"He was connected to what went down in Riverton. I think he's deserving of a conversation with me to answer for it."

"Being connected and being prosecutable are different universes. You know this."

She did know. Had learned it the hard way over years of watching bad people walk free because the system was designed to protect them. But knowing and accepting were different things.

"You sure this is a hill worth dying on?" Banyan asked. "There's always another shadow war brewing. Just saying ... pick your battles."

"Maybe," Hatch said. "But I can't walk away when those responsible for hurting good people go unpunished."

"You can't save the world, Hatch."

"Won't know unless I try."

The silence stretched between them, filled by their brief but dynamic history. Missions that had gone sideways. People they'd saved. People they hadn't. Banyan knew better than pushing when she got like this. Aerosight's demonstration in Riverton had left bodies in its wake. Good people. Someone had to answer for that.

"Fine," he said finally. "Harlan's got a media appearance tomorrow. Some press panel thing, probably pre-screened softball questions, but it'll be public. I'll send you the schedule."

"Appreciate it."

"You're going to do something stupid, aren't you?"

"That depends. You going to try and stop me?"

"Not anymore. Just don't make me clean up after it."

"When have I ever—"

"New Hampshire ring a bell?"

"That was different. Extenuating circumstances."

"What makes this different?"

She took a sip of her coffee sludge. "Don't know."

"I guess in our world, certainty is a commodity in short supply."

The waitress appeared with her food. Eggs that actually looked like they'd seen a chicken, bacon thick as playing cards, hashbrowns crispy enough to use as roof shingles. Hatch nodded her thanks.

"I have to go," she told Banyan. "Breakfast is here."

"Priorities. I respect that. Try not to start any international incidents before lunch."

"No promises."

She ended the call and surveyed her plate. Real food. Not drive-through garbage or energy bars that tasted like compressed sadness. She ate methodically, fueling up for whatever came next. The eggs were perfect. The bacon was even better. It was smoky and complex, like Ginny had promised.

"You look like a woman planning something reckless."

Ginny had materialized again, coffee pot at the ready.

"Only if I miss breakfast," Hatch said.

"Smart. Bad decisions are worse on an empty stomach." She topped off the mug. "You military?"

The question caught Hatch off-guard. "Once upon a time."

"Could tell. Way you sit. Way you watch the room. My boy came back from Afghanistan doing the same thing. Took him two years to stop checking corners."

"He doing okay now?"

"Better. Got himself a job, a girl, a mortgage. Normal problems." Ginny's smile was tired but genuine. "Sometimes that's all you can ask for."

Normal problems. Hatch tried to imagine it. Worrying about interest rates instead of interrogation techniques. Planning vacations instead of infiltration routes. The thought felt as foreign as a different language.

Her phone buzzed. New message.

"I'll let you get back to your meal," Ginny said, reading the room. "Holler if you need anything."

Hatch flipped open the phone. Banyan had already come through, as always. A PDF attachment with Harlan's schedule for the next week. She scrolled to tomorrow's entry:

2:00 PM

National Press Building, Washington D.C.

Event: "Inside the Beltway: A National Security Roundtable with Congressman William Harlan."

Topic: "Emerging Threats in the Digital Age."

The irony was thick enough to choke on. The man who'd helped orchestrate a town's digital hostage situation would stand in front of cameras and pretend to be concerned about American safety, relaying the dangers of cyber warfare and infrastructural security.

Hatch sipped her coffee, eyes narrowing as she memorized the details. The National Press Building would have security, but it was also public. Cameras everywhere. Witnesses. Harlan would be on his best behavior, playing the role of dedicated public servant.

But every show had an intermission. Every actor eventually stepped off stage.

She pulled up a map on her phone. D.C. was three hours north, maybe less if she pushed it. Plenty of time to scout the location, identify his likely routes, figure out where a congressman might go when he thought no one was watching.

The diner had started to fill up. Morning shifters for some local factory, by the looks of them. Men and women in work clothes, grabbing coffee and calories before another day on the line. Real people with real problems, unaware that men like Kern and Harlan played games with their lives from boardrooms and back channels.

Hatch left cash on the table, enough for the meal and a decent tip. Ginny caught her eye from behind the counter, and gave a small nod. One survivor recognizing another.

Outside, the morning had sharpened into focus. The sun climbed higher, burning off the highway mist. Her Jeep waited, patient as an old dog. She'd need to find a place to clean up, maybe grab a few hours of real sleep before tomorrow. But first, she had homework to do. Research. Reconnaissance. The unglamorous parts of the job that movies always skipped.

She climbed in, tossing her jacket on the passenger seat. Her cell phone vibrated. Hatch looked at the incoming number and the Colorado area code. She sat for a moment before picking it up.

"Hi mom."

"Didn't think you'd answer. Didn't even know if this number still worked. You change them so often."

"Everything okay?"

"Can't a mom check in on her daughter without there being some crisis?"

Hatch wasn't sure how to answer. She'd spent the majority of her adult life away from her childhood home. Only the death of her twin sister had brought her back into the fold. In the time since, she'd rebuilt the fractured relationship with her mother. Although foreign to her, Hatch guessed that this is what normal families do. She was grateful when her mom continued the conversation in her silence.

"I just worry about you sometimes. That's all."

"I'm fine. No need to worry." Hatch could tell from the huff on the other end that her mother wasn't satisfied.

"I'll just feel better once you're home again."

"Not much longer. Just wrapping up some loose ends on something I'm working on."

"Good. Because I don't think I could bear the look on Daphne's face if you're not here for her birthday."

"I promised. I keep my promises." Hatch's ten-year-old niece had forced her into a binding verbal contract the way that only kids can do. "I'll be there."

"Well, we can't wait to see you. I miss you."

"Be there before you know it." Hatch was never good with the sentimental. "I've gotta run. Give the kids a kiss for me and give Jed my regards."

"You be safe out there. It's a crazy world."

Hatch knew better than most the truth of her words. "See you in a week or so." She ended the call.

The engine turned over on the second try. Not bad for a vehicle held together by rust and spite. As she pulled out of the lot, she glanced one more time at Harlan's schedule on her phone, refocusing her mind to the task at hand.

"Let's see what the congressman has to say when the cameras stop rolling."

THREE

THE MAKEUP GIRL'S HANDS WERE SOFT AS A WHISPERED prayer, dabbing foundation across Congressman William Harlan's forehead. She couldn't have been more than twenty-three, fresh out of some communications program, still bright-eyed about working in the nation's capital. Still naive enough to think proximity to power meant something.

"Almost done, Congressman," she said, leaning in to blend a spot near his temple. Her perfume was something floral, young, trying too hard.

Harlan caught her wrist. Gentle. Just enough pressure to make her pause. "You know, Sarah—"

"It's Sandra."

"Sandra." He let the name roll off his tongue like he was tasting wine. "You have remarkable hands. Steady. Delicate. I bet you're good at all sorts of things."

She went still, the makeup sponge hovering between them. Her smile tightened at the corners—the look of someone realizing the room had suddenly gotten smaller.

"Just makeup, Congressman." She pulled her hand free, professional mask sliding into place. "Let me get the powder. Don't want you looking shiny under those lights."

She retreated to the counter, putting blessed distance between them. Harlan watched her in the mirror, noting the way her shoulders had drawn up, defensive. The way she wouldn't meet his eyes anymore.

His security detail—Morrison, six-foot-three of compressed violence in a black suit—stood by the door like a statue. Harlan caught his eye, gave a slight shrug that said *Can't blame a man for trying*.

"They're all too sensitive these days," he muttered, loud enough for Morrison to hear but quiet enough to maintain plausible deniability if Sandra complained. Which she wouldn't. They never did. Not if they wanted to keep working in this town.

A knock at the door saved everyone from further discomfort. A producer poked her head in—late thirties, clipboard clutched like a life preserver, stress radiating from every pore.

"One minute, Congressman. We need you in position."

Harlan stood, smoothing his tie—red silk, exactly the right shade to pop on camera without looking aggressive. Image was everything. Had been since his first campaign twenty years ago, when he'd learned that voters didn't want truth. They wanted performance.

"Lead the way."

The walk to the studio floor was a familiar parade. Interns scattered like minnows before a shark. Junior staffers tried to look busy and important. The whole building hummed with that particular D.C. energy—ambition and anxiety in equal measure, everyone desperate to matter.

#HarlanLive trending at 47K tweets, Harlan noted, glancing at the social media monitor in the hallway.

Good. Strong engagement numbers.

The set was pure political theater. Soft lighting made everyone look ten years younger. Backdrop of leather-bound books no one had ever read. American flag positioned just so in the corner, subtle but present. Like democracy itself—visible enough to reassure, distant enough not to interfere with business.

Evan Reade was already seated, reviewing notes on his tablet. Mid-forties, silver at the temples, one of those journalists who'd made a career of seeming tough while never quite drawing blood. Safe enough to book big names, dangerous enough to maintain credibility.

He stood as Harlan approached, professional smile in place. "Congressman. Thanks for making time."

They shook hands. Harlan's grip was firm, held a beat too long. Then he pulled Reade closer, voice dropping to a whisper that wouldn't reach the boom mics.

"Blindside me with some bullshit and I promise this'll be the last interview of your career."

Reade's smile never wavered, but his eyes hardened. "Noted."

Harlan released him, switching seamlessly to his public face—warm, confident, a servant of the people. He settled into his chair as the crew made final adjustments. A tech clipped a wireless mic to his lapel, fingers careful not to muss the silk.

"Sound check?" she asked.

"Testing, one two three. The rain in Spain falls mainly on the plain."

"Perfect. We're live in three, two ..." The final count came as a raised finger, then nothing. The red light bloomed to life.

"Good morning," Reade began, voice shifting into his broadcast register. "I'm Evan Reade, and today we're discussing America's infrastructure vulnerabilities with Congressman William Harlan, Chairman of the House Subcommittee on Cybersecurity. Congressman, thank you for joining us."

"Always a pleasure, Evan."

And they were off, dancing through the familiar steps. Harlan had done this routine a hundred times. Express concern about threats. Emphasize the need for private-public partnerships. Drop in some folksy wisdom about Main Street values. Never get specific enough to be pinned down later.

He's playing it safe. Harlan watched Reade telegraph his questions with subtle shifts in posture. *Staying in the shallow end.*

The chyron at the bottom of the screen read: *CYBER THREATS:*

HOW VULNERABLE IS AMERICA? Perfect framing. Made him look like the defender, not the profiteer.

CNN BREAKING: Infrastructure spending bill faces resistance in Senate ...

" ...which brings us to the recent events in Riverton, Texas." Reade's voice had taken on a different quality. Sharper. Like a knife being drawn from its sheath.

Harlan had been expecting this. Had rehearsed his response in the car, refined it with his communications director, polished it until it gleamed.

"A real tragedy," he said, letting genuine-seeming sorrow color his voice. "What happened in Riverton is exactly why this new contract with AeroSight is so crucial. We're finally bringing twenty-first-century infrastructure defense to Main Street America. Companies like AeroSight represent the best of American innovation—private enterprise stepping up to protect our communities."

Spin the tragedy into necessity. Make AeroSight the solution, not the problem.

"But isn't it true, Congressman, that you stand to profit directly from this contract?" Reade leaned forward. "You own shares in AeroSight, correct?"

There it was. The ambush. Harlan felt his jaw tighten, muscles clenching involuntarily. But he'd been in politics too long to let it show beyond that micro-expression. His smile remained steady, though something cold flickered behind his eyes.

Conflict of interest angle. Predictable but effective. Time for the full-disclosure defense.

"I've owned shares in dozens of American companies, Evan. I was a businessman long before I entered public service. AeroSight happened to be one of many investments I saw potential in years ago. And frankly? I'm proud that a company I believed in is now in a position to serve our national security interests."

"Some might say that's a conflict of interest."

"Some might say a lot of things." Harlan's voice carried just a hint of steel now. "But my financial disclosures have always been transparent. Every investment, every holding, filed according to ethics guidelines. What I find interesting is that we're discussing my portfolio instead of discussing how to protect American cities from cyber attacks."

"Fair point, Congressman." Reade knew when to retreat. "Let's talk about that protection ..."

The rest was autopilot. Talking points about hardening the grid, protecting water systems, the need for vigilance. Harlan could deliver this speech in his sleep. Actually had at a dozen fundraisers.

Twitter engagement up 23% since the conflict question, he noted, catching a glimpse of the producer's screen. *Controversy drives clicks. Always has.*

Finally, mercifully, Reade wrapped up. "Congressman Harlan, thank you for your time."

"Thank you, Evan."

The red light died. The performance ended. Instantly, the set's energy shifted from staged warmth to barely concealed hostility.

Harlan was on his feet before the tech could unclip his mic. He rounded on Reade, voice low and dangerous.

"What the hell was that last shot?"

Reade was already gathering his notes, unimpressed. "Just doing my job."

"You'll be doing it from Nowheresville, Missouri, by next week. I'll see to that."

For the first time, Reade's smile was genuine. "You're not the first to make that threat."

"That wasn't a threat." Harlan stepped closer, using his height advantage. "I don't make threats. I make promises. Ask around."

He stalked off toward the green room, yanking at his tie like it was strangling him. Sandra reappeared with removal wipes. He snatched them from her hand.

"I've got it."

Morrison stepped into the room, closing the door behind him. The ambient studio chatter seemed to fade, as if the building itself was holding its breath. Morrison's shoulders had drawn up almost imperceptibly—the stance of a man whose threat radar had just started pinging.

"Sir? Someone here to see you."

Harlan didn't look up from the mirror. "Unless it's the President himself, they can make an appointment."

"I think you'll want to see him."

Something in Morrison's tone made Harlan pause. He followed his security chief's gaze to the back corner of the room, where shadows gathered despite the overhead fluorescents.

David Kern stepped forward. Just enough to be seen. Not enough for anyone else to catch him through the door's window.

"Jesus Christ," Harlan muttered. Then, louder, "Give us the room."

Morrison hesitated, but Harlan's glare brooked no argument. The door clicked shut.

"Hallway," Kern said. One word. An order disguised as a suggestion.

They moved to a service corridor, away from the studio's main traffic. Concrete walls and exposed pipes, the building's ugly bones hidden from public view. It smelled of industrial cleaner and old coffee.

"You should know better than to show up unannounced," Harlan hissed. "Bad enough the press is sniffing around Riverton. We can't be seen together."

"Nobody saw me." Kern's voice was calm as a frozen lake. "Nobody does unless I want them to."

"So what was so urgent it couldn't wait for a secure call?"

"We have a problem."

Harlan felt his stomach tighten. In his experience, when men like Kern said "problem," they meant "catastrophe."

"Riverton?"

Kern shook his head. "No. A leak."

"Then it's your problem."

Kern's expression didn't change, but the temperature in the hallway seemed to drop five degrees. "My problems are your problems. If my ship sinks, I'll make damn sure you're on board when it goes down."

The threat hung between them like a blade. Harlan had made his own fortune before politics and had climbed over plenty of bodies to reach his current perch. But Kern was different. Kern was the kind of man who didn't climb over bodies. He made them disappear like they'd never even existed.

"So what's the leak?"

"We have a whistleblower. One of our scientists. Dr. Samuel Carter." Kern paused, letting the name sink in. "He created the Rift prototype. When he finally understood what it could really do, he developed a conscience. Decided the world needed to know."

Harlan processed this, his mind already calculating angles and exposures. "You mean the project that creates earthquakes?"

"To put it bluntly, yes."

"Christ." Harlan ran a hand through his hair, probably undoing an hour of styling. "How many people know?"

"Just the reporter he planned to share the files with."

"And the reporter?"

"Had a tragic drowning accident early this morning. The Potomac can be treacherous this time of year."

Harlan nodded slowly. He didn't need details. Didn't want them. "And Carter?"

"He's scheduled to meet a "substitute" journalist tomorrow. After that meeting ..." Kern spread his hands. "Problem solved."

"Probably best I don't know more. Plausible deniability."

Kern's smile was thin as a razor. "That's exactly why I'm making sure you do know. Plausible deniability only works if you've been properly warned about what you're denying."

The bastard's boxing me in. Making sure that if the operation goes sideways, I can't claim ignorance. Mutual assured destruction—we rise or fall together, bound by mutual blackmail as much as business interests.

"Just make sure it all goes away," Harlan said aloud.

"I always do."

They stood there. The fluorescent lights hummed overhead. Harlan saw in Kern a mirrored reflection of himself. They were architects of necessary evils, builders of a world where might and money were the only metrics that mattered.

The door at the end of the hallway opened. Morrison's head appeared. "Sir? Your reservation at Charlemagne's is in thirty minutes."

Harlan nodded, already shifting back into his public persona. He turned to say something else to Kern, but the hallway was empty. The man had vanished like smoke, leaving only the lingering sense of threat and the smell of expensive cologne.

Harlan straightened his tie, ran fingers through his hair, composed his face into the expression of a dedicated public servant. He had a luncheon to attend. Donors to charm. The machinery of democracy to oil with promises and pork.

But as he walked back toward the studio exit, he couldn't shake the feeling that something had shifted. That the careful balance of power and profit he'd spent decades building was standing on ground that might, at any moment, begin to shake.

Project Rift. Earthquakes on demand. And somewhere out there, a scientist with a conscience was about to meet his end.

Harlan pushed through the studio doors into the D.C. morning. The city sprawled before him—monuments to democracy rising like white teeth from a jaw that could bite down at any moment.

He climbed into his waiting town car, Morrison holding the door before circling around to the driver's seat. The big man folded himself behind the wheel with practiced efficiency—security detail and chauffeur rolled into one, a cost-cutting measure Harlan had sold as "streamlining" but was really about having fewer people who knew where he went and when.

Harlan settled back into a leather seat that cost more than most Americans made in a month. In the rearview mirror, Morrison's eyes met his for a moment—professional, wary.

Harlan closed his eyes and tried not to think about earthquakes.

Or the ground that might already be shifting beneath his feet.

HATCH SAT ACROSS THE STREET. She watched Congressman Harlan being escorted by his driver into the backseat of a town car. After closing the door, the driver paused and checked his surroundings, scanning the foot traffic before entering the vehicle himself.

She made a mental note. Harlan's driver wasn't just a chauffeur. He was his security guard.

The vehicle pulled out from the curb and into traffic. Hatch waited until a few cars had filled the gap before following.

FOUR

Dr. Samuel Carter stood in the driveway of his Old Town Alexandria rowhouse, watching his breath mist in the cool morning air. Spring was slow in making its appearance this year. He held a bundle of aluminum tent poles as if they might detonate at any moment. The narrow brick-lined street stretched before him in both directions, lined with Federal-style homes that had witnessed two centuries of American history. At seven-thirty on a Saturday morning, the neighborhood held that peculiar quiet of families either sleeping in or already fled to their weekend escapes.

Behind him, the SUV's rear hatch yawned open like a hungry mouth, already half-filled with the detritus of a family attempting to escape civilization for a few days. Coolers, duffel bags, camping chairs, and enough provisions to survive a minor apocalypse created a Jenga puzzle that defied the laws of physics and common sense.

"Sam, honey, the tent poles go in the bag with the tent."

His wife Laura, watched from beside the vehicle, trying not to laugh as he attempted to jam the poles into a duffel bag already bursting with boots and rain gear. Even at this early hour, she looked put-together in that effortless way that had first caught his attention fifteen years ago at a graduate school mixer. She'd pulled her auburn hair back into a practical ponytail and wore the kind of outdoor gear that suggested competence without trying too hard.

"I know that," Carter replied, though it was clear he didn't. The poles seemed determined to spring from his grasp like unruly snakes. "I'm just ... reorganizing."

"You're a geologist, not a survivalist." Laura rescued the poles from his fumbling hands, sliding them into the proper bag with practiced ease. "We're going to a cabin with running water and electricity, not camping on the moon."

Carter felt heat creep up his neck despite the cool morning air. After nearly two decades of marriage, Laura could still make him feel like a graduate student who'd forgotten how to operate basic equipment.

"I just don't want to forget anything important," he said.

"Like bug spray?"

"Like Miles' inhaler."

The words stopped her mid-motion, tent poles forgotten. They both turned toward the house, where their eight-year-old son was making his way down the front steps with the careful deliberation of a child who'd learned that running could trigger a tightness in his chest that made breathing feel like sucking air through a straw.

Miles clutched his stuffed triceratops—a battered green dinosaur named Stomper that had seen him through surgery, hospital stays, and countless nights when his breathing had turned shallow and frightening. In his other hand, he carried his Nintendo Switch, even though his mom had told him this was supposed to be a digital detox weekend.

"Already packed." Laura patted the red medical bag wedged between two coolers, her voice carrying the practiced calm of a mother who'd learned to manage crises without broadcasting panic. "Three of everything. Inhaler, nebulizer, emergency meds, backup nebulizer, and another backup for the backup. Unless we want to explain to a medevac pilot why we thought two of anything would be enough."

Carter's shoulders relaxed slightly. In the controlled environment of his Georgetown University lab, he could predict seismic stress patterns within hundredths of a percent. He could isolate variables, measure outcomes, replicate results. But out here in the real world—the world where his son's airways could close from a single whiff of the wrong pollen or a shift in barometric pressure—nothing felt certain.

Miles reached the SUV, already winded from the twenty-foot walk. His pale complexion held that translucent quality that always worried Carter, even though the pediatric pulmonologist insisted this was normal for children with persistent asthma. Miles had already spent more time in hospitals than most adults, yet he maintained the resilient optimism that seemed hardwired into children who'd learned early on that life was fragile but still worth living.

"Dad, does the cabin have Wi-Fi?" Miles asked, clutching his Switch like a lifeline.

"Nope," Laura answered before Carter could construct a diplomatic lie. "It has trees, and squirrels, and the world's slowest card games."

Miles' face crumpled into an existential despair only an eight-year-old could muster. "That's child abuse."

"That's called vacation." Laura ruffled his sandy hair, which stuck up at angles that defied both gravity and styling products. "Go grab your backpack. The one with your books, not the one full of candy I'm pretending not to know about."

"The candy is for emergencies," Miles protested, trudging back toward the house. "Like boredom. Or bears."

"Bears don't eat candy, sweetie."

"Then why are they always trying to steal picnic baskets?"

Carter watched his son disappear through the front door, muttering what sounded like a child's interpretation of constitutional law and the Geneva Convention. Despite the weight of the secrets he carried, the growing certainty that his life's work had been perverted into something monstrous, Miles could still make him smile.

He pulled out his phone for what felt like the hundredth time that morning. The message thread with Ethan Voss stared back at him, the last exchange from two days ago burned into his memory:

Still on for Sunday morning?

Wouldn't miss it. This is too important.

But nothing since then. No confirmation. No last-minute details. No characteristic flood of rhetoric about exposing corporate malfeasance and protecting the innocent. Just an ominous silence that grew heavier with each passing hour.

Carter's thumbs moved across the screen:

Heading out to the cabin now. I'll see you at the spot tomorrow morning.

He hit send, watched the status change to "Delivered," then waited. The morning air carried the scent of woodsmoke from someone's fireplace and the distant hum of weekend traffic building on the nearby interstate. A jogger passed, earbuds in, lost in whatever rhythm carried her through the Alexandria streets.

His phone buzzed.

See you then.

Carter stared at the response, unease coiling in his stomach like a parasite. The reply was wrong in ways he couldn't quite articulate. Too brief. Too formal. Devoid of the passionate intensity that characterized everything Ethan Voss said or wrote. The journalist who'd spent forty-five minutes on the phone describing the moral imperative of exposing corporate corruption didn't communicate in three-word responses.

But Carter was already too deep to back out now. The thumb drive in his satchel contained three months of carefully collected evidence—technical specifications, internal memos, email chains where AeroSight executives discussed casualty projections with the clinical detachment of accountants reviewing quarterly reports. Tomorrow morning, he'd hand it all over to someone who could transform it from a dangerous secret into public knowledge.

Maybe then he could sleep without dreaming of San Francisco's skyline collapsing into the Bay, or Los Angeles sliding into the Pacific as artificial earthquakes tore the state apart along fault lines that were never meant to bear that kind of stress.

"If I didn't know you better, I'd think you were having an affair with that screen."

Laura's voice cut through his spiraling thoughts. He looked up to find her watching him with an expression she reserved for moments when his absent-minded professor routine crossed the line into actual worry. Her green eyes held that mixture of affection and concern that had anchored him through graduate school, through the lean years of fighting for tenure, through every crisis that had tested their marriage.

"Huh? What?"

"Classic guilt response." She was teasing, but Carter caught the flicker of real concern beneath her humor. After two decades together, Laura could read his moods like seismograph recordings. "Everything okay?"

"It's just work stuff." The lie came easier than it should have, polished smooth by three months of practice. Three months of carrying the weight of knowledge that could topple governments or trigger the kind of geological catastrophe that would make 9/11 look like a small-town car accident.

He'd told himself it was protection—that keeping Laura and Miles ignorant of what he'd discovered would keep them safe. But late at night, when the house was quiet and his conscience was loud, he knew the truth. He was protecting himself from the look that would replace the love in her eyes if she knew what he'd helped create.

"Sam?" Her voice pulled him back from the edge of the abyss. "You sure you're okay?"

"Yeah." He managed what he hoped was a convincing smile. "Just ready to unplug for a few days."

"Good. Because I already told Miles you'd teach him to fish."

"I don't know how to fish."

"Then you'll learn together. Character building." Laura's grin held the satisfaction of a woman who'd just solved two problems with one solution. "Besides, watching you try to bait a hook will be worth the price of admission."

Despite the weight pressing against his chest, Carter felt something loosen inside him. Laura had a gift for making everything in the world feel normal.

The satchel. He'd left it on the kitchen counter.

"Be right back," he said, jogging toward the house.

Inside, morning light slanted through the windows of their small kitchen, illuminating the organized chaos of a family preparing for escape. Coffee cups in the sink, Miles' vitamins arranged in a weekly dispenser, Laura's mystery novel bookmarked and waiting on the counter beside his leather satchel.

The bag sat where he'd left it, worn smooth by fifteen years of conferences and field work. Carter had carried it through geological surveys in Wyoming, academic presentations in Brussels, and collaborative research sessions that had seemed so important at the time. Now, it contained the most dangerous information on Earth.

He flipped it open, performing his ritual inventory check. The thumb drive nestled in its protective case, innocuous as a house key. The folder of printouts was thick with technical diagrams labeled "RIFT WAVE GENERATOR v3.1" and internal memos discussing "controlled seismic events" and "infrastructure stress testing."

One page had worked loose from the stack—a map of the United States overlaid with red circles marking dormant fault lines. Potential target zones. Cities like San Francisco, Los Angeles, and Seattle, where millions of residents went about their daily lives, unaware of their presence on David Kern's chess board.

Carter's hands shook as he closed the satchel and fastened the buckles tight. In twelve hours, this would all be over. The weight of knowledge would transfer from his shoulders to someone else's, someone with the platform and courage to turn secrets into headlines.

"Sam!" Laura's voice carried through the open window. "We need to go if we want to beat the weekend traffic!"

"Coming!"

He grabbed the bag and headed for the door, nearly colliding with Miles in the narrow hallway. His son had returned with a backpack that bulged suspiciously and what appeared to be a small telescope.

"Dad, can I bring my microscope too?"

"To the mountains?"

"There might be cool rocks." Miles' eyes held a brightness that meant he'd discovered something fascinating. "Did you know that the Appalachians are some of the oldest mountains in the world? They're like, four hundred million years old. That's older than dinosaurs."

His son's passion for science had emerged early, manifesting as endless questions about how the world worked and why. In better circumstances, Carter might have nurtured that curiosity into a career in geology or physics. Now, he found himself hoping Miles would choose something safer. Accounting, maybe. Or art history.

"Sure, buddy. But you carry it."

They finished loading the SUV with the systematic efficiency of a family that had learned to travel with medical equipment, emergency supplies, and enough redundancy to handle whatever crisis might emerge in the wilderness. Miles' microscope joined Laura's stack of paperback mysteries, Carter's geological survey maps, and enough food to feed a small expedition.

Carter wedged his satchel behind the driver's seat, trying to look casual about the placement while ensuring it would be within reach if needed. The weight of it seemed to press against his spine through the seat back.

Laura noticed anyway. She always noticed.

"Sam."

"What?"

Her voice carried that patient tone she used when Miles tried to negotiate bedtime extensions. "You promised. No work. This is supposed to be family time."

"It's just some light grading. Midterm papers. I'll leave it in the car, I promise."

She gave him the look—the one that said she wasn't buying his explanation but was choosing to let it slide for the sake of domestic peace. Marriage, Carter reflected, was built on such small mercies and strategic blindnesses.

"Fine," Laura said. "But if I catch you sneaking out to the car at midnight with a flashlight, I'm throwing that bag in the lake."

"There's no lake at the cabin."

"There's a river."

They climbed into the SUV, Miles already plugging his Nintendo Switch into the charging port. The vehicle groaned under the weight of their temporary exodus from civilization.

Carter turned the key, listening to the engine settle into its familiar rhythm. He checked the mirrors with the excessive caution of a man who spent his professional life studying how solid ground could suddenly betray you without warning. The neighborhood looked normal in the early morning light—joggers and dog walkers beginning their weekend routines, newspapers waiting on doorsteps, the comfortable predictability of suburban Saturday morning.

As they pulled out of the driveway, Carter caught sight of a black sedan parked three houses down. Nothing remarkable about it—government-issued bland, the kind car rental agencies bought by the thousand. But something about it gnawed at him.

He'd seen the same car, or one very much like it, parked near the university two days ago. And again yesterday, outside the grocery store where he'd stopped to stock up on road trip snacks.

Carter shrugged it off. Probably nothing. The D.C. area was full of black sedans driven by bureaucrats and contractors and the anonymous machinery of the federal government. He hushed the paranoia and focused on the road ahead.

The Alexandria streets were Saturday-quiet, painted in the soft light of early morning. They passed familiar landmarks that marked the geography of their family life—the old stone church where they'd attended exactly one service before deciding they were "spiritual but not religious," the small park where Miles had suffered his first serious asthma attack and Carter had experienced real terror for the first time in his life, watching his child fight for breath.

There was the Starbucks where Carter had first met Ethan Voss six months ago, back when Project Rift was nothing more than suspicious data patterns and growing unease. The journalist had been everything Carter expected—passionate, idealistic, convinced that truth was a weapon powerful enough to cut through corporate conspiracy and government corruption.

Now, judging by that black sedan just a few cars behind them, Carter deduced that Voss was probably dead, and Carter was driving toward a meeting that might just be his own execution.

"We need to get there before dark," he said as they merged onto

495, the familiar rhythm of highway driving beginning to settle his nerves. "Cell service gets spotty in the mountains. Don't want to be navigating by fireflies."

"The GPS will work," Laura said, already settling into her mystery novel.

"The GPS thinks there's a road where there's actually a creek bed. Trust me, I checked the geological surveys." Carter glanced in the rearview mirror. Three cars back, maintaining perfect distance, the black sedan had joined the flow of weekend traffic. "I always check the geological surveys."

"Of course you did." Laura's hand found his on the gear shift, warm and reassuring. "It's going to be good, Sam. All of us together. No screens, no schedules, no—"

"No cell service," Miles groaned from the backseat, already absorbed in his handheld game.

"You'll survive. People lived for thousands of years without Instagram."

"Yeah, and they all died of dysentery."

"That's on the Oregon Trail, not real life."

"Same thing."

Carter let his family's familiar banter wash over him, the comfortable rhythm of conversation that had sustained them through years of small crises and quiet victories.

By the time they reached the first toll plaza, Miles had fallen asleep despite his protests about digital detox, his breathing wheezy but regular. Laura had opened her paperback—something involving a detective with personal demons and a murder in a small English village—and was already reading particularly pertinent passages aloud for Carter's amusement.

"*Detective Montgomery's piercing blue eyes penetrated her very soul,*" she read in a dramatically breathy voice.

"That's physically impossible," Carter said, checking the mirrors again. The sedan was still there, maintaining a careful distance. "Eyes don't penetrate. They reflect light."

"You're ruining the magic of bad romance."

"Sorry. Occupational hazard."

The city fell away behind them as they climbed into the foothills of the Blue Ridge Mountains. Suburbs gave way to farmland, then forest, as the road wound higher into country that remembered older rhythms. The trees wore their autumn colors like a celebration—gold and scarlet and deep orange that seemed to glow with internal fire.

The Blue Ridge Mountains rose in the distance, ancient and patient, formed by geological forces that made human concerns seem ephemeral as mayflies. Carter had studied these mountains, knew their composition and history, understood the slow dance of tectonic pressure that had lifted them from prehistoric seabeds into the sky.

But today, seeing their timeless profiles against the morning clouds, he felt only the weight of what he carried and the certainty that tomorrow would change everything.

In the rearview mirror, the black sedan maintained its careful pursuit, neither gaining nor falling back, patient as the mountains themselves.

FIVE

D.C. TRAFFIC WAS ITS OWN SPECIAL CIRCLE OF HELL. Hatch sat three cars back from Congressman William Harlan's black town car, watching brake lights bloom red in the afternoon glare. The congressman's car hadn't moved more than fifty feet in the last five minutes. Perfect. In gridlock this thick, maintaining a tail was like following a glacier—technically possible, but requiring the patience of stone.

She kept her Jeep in the right lane, letting aggressive Uber drivers and harried Hill staffers provide natural cover. Harlan's driver—Gary Morrison, according to Banyan's intel—was competent enough to check mirrors, but not paranoid enough to spot a tail who knew how to breathe with the traffic.

The sedan's blinker flashed. Left turn ahead. Hatch waited two beats before signaling the same. Let a BMW squeeze between them. Distance was her friend. In the city, three car lengths might as well be three miles when it came to staying invisible.

Hatch's phone buzzed on the console. Banyan, probably, wanting an update. She ignored it. You didn't text and tail. You picked one and committed.

Harlan finally made the turn, sliding into the kind of neighborhood where restaurants didn't need signs because everyone who mattered already knew where they were. Old money streets lined with trees older than the republic and townhouses that whispered about senators and their secrets.

She watched the sedan glide between parked Audis and Teslas, eventually pulling up to a building that might have been a private residence if not for the discrete valet stand. No sign. No name. Just tinted windows and a door that suggested you either belonged or you didn't.

Charlemagne's. Hatch had heard of it. The kind of place where defense contractors ate fifty-dollar appetizers while discussing hundred-million-dollar contracts. Where committee chairs made promises that shaped policy and ruined lives, all between the soup course and the fish.

She circled the block twice before finding a spot with a partial view of the entrance. Two blocks down, wedged between a florist van and somebody's abandoned Vespa. Not ideal, but workable. Hatch pulled her compact Steiner binoculars from the glove box—military grade, a gift from her former life that kept on giving.

Through the magnified view, she watched Harlan enter the building. Morrison stayed with the car, fending off a young valet offering to park it for him. This little stop wasn't on the itinerary Banyan had given her.

Ten minutes passed. Twenty. Hatch settled into the familiar rhythm of surveillance. The trick was to stay alert without staying tense. To watch without watching. Let the mind drift just enough to keep from going stir-crazy, but never so far that you missed the critical moment.

A small hatchback with a blue Uber light illuminating the dash pulled up. A woman stepped out from the back. Harlan's security man walked over to greet her. A small verbal exchange. Hatch gauged the woman to be in her late twenties, maybe early thirties. The kind of beauty that took effort but pretended to be effortless. Definitely not Mrs. Harlan, whose photos Hatch had reviewed. The congressman's wife was fifteen years older and preferred pantsuits to cocktail dresses.

The woman disappeared inside. The driver then got into the town car and pulled it into a parking spot marked VIP. He remained in the vehicle.

Hatch adjusted the binoculars, found an angle through the tinted glass. There—corner table. Harlan stood as the woman approached. Kissed her cheek, but his hand lingered on her lower back a beat too long for professional courtesy.

Campaign donors don't get that look. Neither do spouses, past a certain age.

She lowered the binoculars. It didn't matter who Harlan was screwing. Half of D.C. was cheating on the other half. Musical beds among the powerful. What mattered were the patterns. Vulnerabilities. Moments when the man's guard came down.

Hatch's stomach growled, reminding her that surveillance required fuel. A food truck sat at the corner, one of those gourmet taco operations that charged eight dollars for something that should cost two. She locked the Jeep, walked over, ordered black coffee and whatever they recommended.

"Long day?" the vendor asked, noting her thousand-yard stare.

"Getting longer."

"I hear that. You a cop?"

"Something like that."

He handed her a wrapped taco and the coffee. "On the house. You look like you're doing something important."

"Just watching the world go by."

"In this town? That's a full-time job."

She walked back to her Jeep, ate standing up, eyes never leaving Charlemagne's entrance. The taco was better than expected. Small miracles.

Surveillance is ninety percent stillness and ten percent lightning. You have to be ready for both.

An hour crawled by. The sun sank lower, painting the brownstones gold. Morrison had gotten out twice to stretch, and walk a small circle around the sedan. Bored. Complacent. The kind of security that was more about status than safety.

Finally, movement. Harlan emerged with the woman on his arm. The driver immediately exited the vehicle. He walked to the passenger side of the town car and held the door open. The woman entered first, followed by the congressman. The driver then circled back and got in. He pulled the car away from the curb.

Hatch counted to five, then followed.

Evening traffic was lighter but still thick enough to hide in. She kept pace, never directly behind, sometimes parallel on side streets. The route suggested routine rather than caution. This was good news for Hatch. Routine was surveillance's best friend.

They headed northwest, away from the federal center. Past the last of the monuments and museums, into the transitional neighborhoods where D.C. tried to pretend it was just another American city.

The town car finally pulled into a hotel entrance. The Whitmore. Nice enough to impress, discrete enough to avoid the gossip columns. The kind of place where powerful men brought women who weren't their wives and nobody asked questions.

She drove past, circled back, and found a spot in the shadow of a parking garage. Through the binoculars, she watched Harlan exit with the woman. He was carrying a briefcase now—leather, expensive, and not something he'd walked in with. In Hatch's experience, briefcases that appeared during dinner usually contained items, information, that couldn't be discussed over an email or phone call. The driver transitioned into the role of security, following a respectful distance behind.

Three players. One principal, one unknown, one guard dog.

She gave them a two-minute head start, then walked into the hotel. The lobby was all modern minimalism—marble and mood lighting, designed to suggest luxury without actually providing it. The elevator was just closing. She caught a glimpse of Harlan's gray suit before the doors sealed.

The floor indicator climbed. Seventh. Eighth. Ninth. Stopped.

The bar beckoned from the left side of the lobby. Dark wood, amber lighting, the kind of place where deals got made and sealed with expensive whiskey. She drifted that way, playing the part of a tired traveler in need of a drink.

The security man sat at the bar's far end, tie loosened, whiskey already half gone. He'd positioned himself to watch the lobby, but his attention was more on his drink than his duty. His jacket hung open, revealing the slight bulge of a shoulder holster. Sloppy. Professional security kept their weapons concealed even when they thought they were safe.

Muscle for rent. The kind of guy who's good with a gun and bad with orders.

She took a seat in the corner, back to the wall, clear sightlines to both the bar and the lobby. The bartender appeared—young, eager, probably working his way through Georgetown.

"What can I get you?" he asked.

"Cranberry juice. Lots of ice."

He didn't blink. In D.C., half the people drinking alone were either alcoholics or on duty. He brought the juice without comment.

Hatch pulled out her phone, scrolled through nothing, occasionally glancing up. Morrison had ordered another whiskey. His shoulders were relaxing, guard dropping with each sip. In the reflection of the bar mirror, she could see him checking his own phone. Probably figured his principal was settled in for the night.

Time stretched like taffy. The bar filled and emptied with the rhythm of hotel life. Business travelers comparing horror stories. A bachelorette party that had started somewhere else and would end somewhere worse. Through it all, Harlan's security drank, and Hatch waited.

That's what wolves do. Wait for the herd to show weakness.

Her phone buzzed. Banyan again. This time she answered the text: *Working. Update later.*

His response was immediate: *Don't do anything I wouldn't do.*

That leaves plenty of options.

Exactly why I'm worried.

Hatch pocketed the phone. She heard the bartender call the security man by name. Morrison was on whiskey number four now. His eyes had that glassy look of a man who'd decided his shift was essentially over. Upstairs, Harlan was doing whatever congressmen did with their mistresses. The briefcase was probably sitting in a corner, forgotten until morning.

Hatch sipped her cranberry juice and let the ambiance wash over her. She'd learned long ago that the key to hunting wasn't speed. It was patience. Persistence. Being there when the moment finally came.

And it would come. It always did.

Harlan thought he was safe. Thought his money and position and drunken security guard were enough to keep the wolves at bay. But he'd already made the fatal mistake.

He'd separated himself from the herd.

Now all she had to do was wait for him to realize it.

SIX

MORRISON'S PHONE LIT UP ON THE BAR LIKE A SUMMONS from God. Or at least from someone who thought he was. Hatch watched in the bar mirror as the security man checked the message, drained the last of his whiskey, and slapped cash on the bar.

"Time to earn my paycheck," he muttered to the bartender.

The bartender—a guy who'd clearly seen Morrison's routine before—grinned. "Don't take too long. She tips better than you do."

"Everyone tips better than me."

"True. But she smells nicer too."

Morrison gave him a mock salute and headed for the elevators, his gait carrying that special wobble of a man who thought he was less drunk than he was. Four whiskeys in an hour. Not fall-down drunk but impaired. The kind of impaired that made reaction times sluggish and judgment calls questionable.

Hatch counted to ten, left money for her cranberry juice, and slipped out of the bar. The elevators were to the right. The stairs to the left. She went left.

Hotel stairwells were all the same—concrete and metal and an echo that made every footstep sound like judgment. She took them two at a time, her boots surprisingly quiet on the industrial carpet.

She reached the ninth-floor landing and eased the door open a crack. Perfect timing. The elevator dinged its arrival. Morrison stepped out, checking his phone again, oblivious to the stairwell door ten feet away.

He walked to a room and knocked—three raps, pause, two more. A code. Cute.

The door opened. The young woman emerged first, hair not quite as perfect as before, lipstick freshly applied but smudged at one corner. She was sliding her phone into her purse, trying to look like she hadn't just been doing what everyone knew she'd been doing.

Morrison stood aside to let her pass. Through the gap, Hatch caught Harlan's voice, casual as if he was dismissing a secretary. "Drop her off and be back in thirty. Give or take traffic."

"Yes, sir."

The door closed. Morrison and the woman headed for the elevator, her heels tapping on the hallway carpet, his steps heavy and unsteady. Neither looked back.

Hatch waited until the elevator doors closed, then slipped into the hallway. Room 917 was halfway down on the right. She needed access, and she needed it quietly.

She moved to Room 917, pulled out a prepaid credit card and started swiping at the lock. Made sure to miss the reader, jabbing at it like someone who'd had one too many.

"Come on," she slurred to no one. "Stupid f—"

She prepared to knock, to play the drunk party girl who'd lost her way when the elevator dinged.

Her pulse spiked. Morrison. Had to be. Forgot something. Saw something. Suspected something.

Hatch turned, ready with a drunk tourist smile, and saw—

A maid. Latina, maybe forty, pushing a cart loaded with tiny shampoo bottles and industrial-grade toilet paper. The woman looked tired in that bone-deep way of people who cleaned up after others for a living.

Hatch swayed, really selling it. "Oh thank God. I left my key inside.

Room 917." She gestured vaguely down the hall. "Just ran to grab ice and the door ..." She mimed it closing.

The maid hesitated. Security protocols versus human sympathy. Hatch slipped the credit card away and gave her best embarrassed smile, dropping the drunk act for another ruse. "I'm such an idiot. My husband's gonna kill me. He's probably already asleep."

That did it. The mention of a husband, the universal exhaustion of dealing with forgetful spouses. The maid sighed and pushed her cart aside.

"Just this once," she said, producing a master keycard from her apron.

"You're an angel. A literal angel."

The lock clicked green. The door opened. Hatch slipped inside with a whispered "thank you" and pressed a twenty into the maid's hand. The door closed with a soft click.

The room was dark except for the bathroom light spilling out through a cracked door. The shower was running, full blast from the sound of it. Steam crept along the ceiling like fog.

Hatch moved fast but silently. The suite was exactly what she'd expected. King bed with too many pillows. Minibar that charged twenty dollars for a Snickers. Art that belonged in a dentist's office.

But it was the bed that stopped her cold.

The briefcase sat open on the silk duvet, but it wasn't full of classified documents or USB drives or any of the spy novel clichés she'd half expected. Instead, it looked like someone had robbed a high-end sex shop.

Ball gag. Leather restraints. A mask that belonged in a German nightclub. Various toys in medical-grade silicone. And there, catching the light like a weapon, a chrome-plated dildo that looked heavy enough to brain someone.

That explains the thirty-minute window.

Harlan's suit jacket was draped over a chair. She quickly checked the pockets. Wallet stuffed with cash and cards. House keys. Hotel keycard. A phone, standard government-issued. If he had a burner, it wasn't here.

The shower cut off.

Hatch grabbed the chrome dildo—thing had to weigh two pounds —and positioned herself behind the bathroom door. Water running. Toilet flush. The door opened fully, and Congressman William Harlan stepped out, towel around his waist, another in his hands rubbing his hair dry.

He was humming. "My Girl" by The Temptations, completely off-key.

Hatch stepped behind him and pressed the base of the chrome toy against the back of his skull. Harlan froze mid-hum. The towel in his hands dropped. His whole body went rigid, that primal freeze response when the brain registers cold metal where cold metal shouldn't be.

"Make a sound," Hatch said, "and this room gets a fresh paint job. Hands where I can

see them. No sudden moves. No hero shit."

Harlan lifted his hands slowly, fingers spread. "My wallet's in my jacket. Take whatever—"

"Shut up." She pressed harder, her voice low and steady. "Don't turn around. Don't talk unless I ask you a question. If it goes well, you leave here with your life. Your dignity?" She paused. "Well, that's up for negotiation."

His breath was coming fast now. Fear sweat had already started forming on his skin, mixing with the shower steam. The towel around his waist was slipping.

"I'm going to step back," Hatch said. "You're going to walk to the bed and sit down. Slowly. You try anything stupid, and the maid's going to have a hell of a cleanup tomorrow."

"Okay. Okay. Just ... please."

"Move."

He shuffled forward, hands still up, towel finally giving up and dropping to the floor. He didn't try to grab it. Just kept moving, pale ass on display, until he reached the bed and sat on the edge.

"Stop." She gestured toward the bed. "See those cuffs? Pick them up."

His eyes darted to the leather restraints among the scattered toys. "You can't be serious."

"Do I look like I'm joking?"

He reached for them with shaking hands.

"Good. Now, the desk chair. Sit."

The chair was one of those ergonomic swivel things, all mesh and adjustable arms. He lowered himself into it like it might explode.

"Cuff your left wrist to the left arm of the chair." Her voice was calm, instructional. "Make it tight. I'll be checking."

"This is kidnapping. False imprisonment. You have any idea what—"

"I have an excellent idea," Hatch said. "Do it."

Harlan's eyes went wide, and he fumbled with the restraint, hands clumsy with fear and humiliation. The leather clicked into place.

"Now lean back and put your right hand behind the chair back."

"I can't reach—"

"Find a way. As a congressman who's built his standing through backdoor deals, I'm sure this isn't the first time you've had to squirm your way into position."

He grunted and contorted, threading his arm through the mesh backing. Hatch stepped closer, keeping the chrome toy visible, and secured his right wrist herself. The position left him spread across the chair, vulnerable and ridiculous.

SEVEN

SHE SPUN THE CHAIR TO FACE HER AND PULLED UP another seat, settling in like they were about to have a board meeting. "Comfortable?"

"Go to hell."

"Maybe someday. But not today." She cast the chrome toy onto the bed.

"You're making the biggest mistake of your life." His voice was raw with humiliation and rage. "Do you have any idea who I am? What I can do to you?"

"Better men have tried." Hatch settled back in her chair. "I'm still here."

"I'm a United States Congressman!" Spittle flew from his lips. "You've kidnapped a federal official. The FBI will have you rotting in a supermax before the week's out."

Hatch's smile was all teeth and no warmth. "You planning to tell them you were held at dildo-point? That you're cuffed to a chair with the same restraints you used on that barely legal assistant who just left?"

"Who the hell are you? What's this all about?"

"You've made some bad decisions recently. And I'm the repercussion."

"You're her. The woman from Riverton."

Hatch leaned in. "You plotted to wage an attack on a small town to further your interests. Money over lives. Power over principles."

"If it's money you want, I can cut you in. Plenty to go around."

"You think this is about money? This is about righting a wrong. This is a reckoning."

Harlan's eyes bounced between Hatch and the door. Neither of which provided any solace. "You don't want me. I'm not the one calling the shots. I'm just as much a victim of this as anyone."

"Besides your current state, you don't look like much of a victim to me."

"I didn't want any part of Riverton. But there are powerful things at work here. Players with vested interest to see certain agendas get through the red tape."

"And you got nothing in return?"

Harlan managed to shrug. "This is Washington. Wheels don't move without grease."

"What's the going price for the life of an American citizen these days?" Hatch continued before Harlan could offer a retort. "Because where I come from, it's priceless."

Harlan pondered for a moment. "Okay, so you can't be bought. Then what? What can I offer?"

"Kern."

"He's the one you want anyway. He's the guy pushing his agenda. Dangerous as they come."

"So quick to turn on someone who's padded your bank account seems like bad business to me."

"It's like you said, a line was crossed in Riverton. I've been looking for an angle to break free. To set things right."

"Seems to me like your motivation is a direct result of your current circumstances. And not out of some altruistic need to do the right thing."

"Does it really matter why?" Harlan's voice cracked. "If your goal is vengeance, then aim it well."

"If I'm going to go after Kern, a man that you claim is so dangerous, what would be my angle of attack?" Hatch watched his face closely, gauging each answer carefully. "Congressman, we can do this easy or hard. Easy means you tell me what I want to know, and maybe the photos I took of your current predicament stay private. Hard means ..." She shrugged. "You've got an election coming up. Imagine the attack ads."

"You're bluffing."

She pulled out her phone with her free hand, and showed him the screen. Three photos, crystal clear. The briefcase. The toys. Him stepping out of the bathroom. Time-stamped and location-tagged. "Not to mention the young girl you entered here with. How many other girls like her would come forward once the word gets out?"

"Your word against mine."

"In a world of instant media saturation, does somebody's word really account for much these days? They say a picture's worth a thousand words. I'd say these are worth much more." Hatch put the phone away. "And if you're thinking that you'll find a way to bury me before I have a chance to hit send, think again. Already uploaded them to a secure server. Anything happens to me, they go wide. Every social media platform you can think of will be reposting this until the next big thing hits. Hell, maybe even Fox News. 'Family Values Congressman's Secret Shame.' Has a nice ring to it."

Harlan slumped in the chair. The fight blew out of him like air from a punctured tire.

"And stop looking at the door," Hatch said. "Your security man won't be back for twenty minutes minimum. D.C. traffic's a bitch this time of night."

She waited for his reaction, but he said nothing, didn't meet her eyes. Harlan looked at her. Took in the scar, her steady hands, her eyes that had seen too much and given up on being shocked by any of it.

"Who are you?" he asked.

"Someone who's done playing nice." She leaned forward. "Your move, Congressman. Choose wisely."

Somewhere in the room, the air conditioner kicked on, adding white noise to the silence. Nine floors below, D.C. went about its evening business—deals and dinners, power and pretense.

But up here, all that mattered was a naked congressman, a woman with nothing to lose, and a chrome-plated sex toy that had become the world's most unlikely interrogation tool.

Harlan's mouth opened, then closed. The fury flickered. Red crept up his neck. "You think one person can stop this? It's bigger than you. Bigger than me. You're pissing in the ocean."

"No shame in trying."

The casual dismissal made him strain against the cuffs. The leather creaked but held. Quality merchandise.

"Tell me about AeroSight," Hatch said, switching gears. "About Kern."

Something in her voice—the absolute certainty, the clinical detachment—made him shrink back as much as the restraints allowed.

"Fine." The word came out like pulled teeth. "If you're here, you've already pieced together my connection to AeroSight. And since you were on the ground in Riverton, you've probably figured out what really happened there."

"I want to hear you confirm it."

Harlan sighed, every one of his fifty-eight years etched into his expression. "It's about money. Massive government contracts. The kind that set up companies for decades. But that's not news, is it? You know all this. So why not just go to the press?"

"Without evidence, I'm just another voice crying conspiracy. Lost in the noise."

"Then what do you hope to accomplish with this?" He gestured at himself, at the room, at the whole sordid scene.

"Justice."

He laughed. "And how exactly do you plan on carrying that out?"

"Simple," Hatch said. "You're going to go before Congress and tell them the truth."

The laughter died. "You must be out of your mind."

Hatch didn't smile. Didn't blink.

"I'm serious," Harlan said, desperation creeping in. "You think I can just waltz into a hearing and confess? They'd crucify me. My career, my family, everything—"

"Your wife." Hatch cut him off with a scoff. "She doesn't know about this little hobby, does she? Not sure how she'd feel about you spending quality time with a girl younger than your daughter."

"She'll never believe you."

Hatch cocked her head. "You sure about that? I'm a woman. We have an intuition about these things. Guarantee anything I tell her will register as truth."

Hatch dropped the phone back into her pocket. "Besides, it's not about proof. It's about narrative. As a politician, you should know that better than anyone."

She watched him deflate, his options evaporating like morning mist. When he spoke again, his voice was smaller, calculating a different angle.

"It's Kern." He licked his lips. "He's out of control. Doesn't trust that anything presented for contract has merit without a field test. Riverton was his idea. I tried to stop him, but—"

"But the money was too good to pass up."

A bitter shrug. "It's a lot of money."

"Human lives don't come with a price tag. But you've never been a boots-on-the-ground kind of guy. Never seen firsthand what your decisions cost."

His eyes found the scar on her arm, the one that disappeared under her sleeve, promising more damage hidden from view. "Guessing you have."

She didn't answer. Didn't need to.

"I can give you Kern," Harlan said. "I do that, and those photos disappear?"

"Depends on what you mean by 'give me Kern.'"

Harlan leaned forward as much as the restraints allowed. "There's a whistleblower. Former AeroSight employee. He's planning to expose a project."

"Riverton?"

"Bigger than Riverton."

Hatch kept her face neutral, but her pulse quickened. "And why tell me this? How does this help your situation?"

"Because Kern is going to have him killed. Tomorrow morning."

The room seemed to shrink around them. "And you're telling me this why?"

"Because Kern is too powerful. Too dangerous. I need to cut ties before he drags me down with him. You being here?" He rattled the cuffs. "Clear example of how his operations are starting to unravel. Too many loose ends."

Her head tilted as she evaluated the politician's body language. Tell me about the whistleblower."

"Samuel Carter. One of their top scientists. Developed something ... significant. I don't know all the details." The words tumbled out. "Just that if it leaks, AeroSight is dead in the water. The company, the contracts, everything goes up in smoke."

"And Kern's solution is murder."

"His solution is always murder. Or worse." Harlan's voice dropped. "Carter's supposed to meet a journalist tomorrow. Diner off the Appalachian Trail. Kern's team will intercept. Make him disappear. If that happens, if he silences Carter, then Kern becomes unstoppable."

Hatch studied him, weighing truth against deception. "And what do you get out of this?"

"Freedom. From him, from his leverage. And you go away. Those photos stay buried." A trickle of sweat ran along the congressman's temple. "I'm offering you a chance to stop Kern. Isn't that what you really want? Justice for what happened in Riverton?"

She stood, paced to the window. Nine floors down, D.C. continued its eternal dance of power and corruption. Somewhere out there, a scientist was spending his last night alive unless she acted.

"Fine," Hatch said finally. "If what you're telling me is true, you have a deal."

Relief washed over his face. "The photos?"

"When it's done, they disappear."

"Thank you. Thank—"

"Save it." She turned back to him. "Where exactly is this meeting supposed to happen?"

"Take the mile marker 47 exit. Dawn. Place called Pete's Diner."

"I find out you've lied, there'll be a reckoning."

"Why do this?" Harlan asked. "Why go through all this trouble? You could have walked away from Riverton. Started fresh. Why chase ghosts?"

"Because good people were hurt," Hatch said. "And someone needs to make sure it doesn't go unpunished."

"You some kind of vigilante? Out there righting wrongs?"

"No." She moved toward the door. "Just someone who lives by a code."

Her hand was on the handle when Harlan cleared his throat. "What about me?"

She paused, turned back as if seeing him for the first time. "Good point."

The ball gag was bright red, medical-grade rubber. She grabbed it from the bed, noted his eyes going wide.

"Wait, you can't—"

The gag cut off his protests. She fastened it tight, probably tighter than necessary. His muffled curses followed her as she snapped one final photo.

"If you're telling the truth, we're done. If not ..." She let the threat hang. "Next time, no safe word."

Hatch slipped out of the room, closing the door on Harlan's muffled rage. The hallway was empty, the hotel quiet except for the distant ding of elevators and muted sounds of other lives behind other doors.

His security would be back soon. He'd find his boss in an extremely compromising position. The resulting chaos would keep them both busy while she disappeared into the night.

Tomorrow at dawn, she'd either save an innocent man or walk into

Kern's trap. Either way, it was better than sitting still. Better than letting the guilty prosper while the good lay buried.

The elevator arrived. Somewhere above her, a United States Congressman was learning that power was relative, that dignity was fragile, and that secrets—like photographs—had a way of finding the light.

The lobby was quiet. She walked through it like she belonged, just another guest heading out for a late dinner. The night doorman didn't even look up from his phone.

Outside, D.C. hummed with its usual energy. Hatch breathed deep, tasting exhaust and ambition and the faint promise of rain. Somewhere in the Virginia mountains, a scientist slept unaware that death was coming with the sunrise.

Not if she could help it.

She found her Jeep, climbed in, and started the engine. By dawn, she'd be at mile marker 47, waiting for whatever came next.

Behind her, The Whitmore Hotel stood like a monument to secrets and power. Nine floors up, those secrets were about to become someone else's problem.

Hatch pulled into traffic and headed for the mountains.

She had a location. A time. A name.

Samuel Carter.

EIGHT

For thirty minutes, Congressman William Harlan had been lying on his side on carpet that reeked of industrial cleaner and the accumulated sins of a thousand clandestine meetings. The Whitmore Hotel's premium suites were supposed to provide discretion and comfort in equal measure, but the plush Persian rug now felt like sandpaper against his cheek, every fiber a reminder of how completely his evening had gone to hell.

The ergonomic office chair—imported Italian leather, adjustable lumbar support, the kind of executive furniture that cost more than most people's monthly salary—had become his prison when it had tipped during his desperate attempts at escape. Now he lay twisted at an angle that sent fire through his spine with every breath.

Sweat pooled where his face pressed against the carpet, mixing with the tears of rage and humiliation that he'd finally stopped trying to hold back. The rubber ball gag had transformed his curses into muffled animal sounds—grunts and whines that echoed inside his skull like the death throes of his political career.

This can't be happening. Not to me. Not to a United States Congressman.

His wrists were raw meat where the leather cuffs had cut into flesh during his thrashing. The restraints were his own—top-quality

German leather that he'd special-ordered from a discrete supplier in Berlin. Ironic that his taste for expensive bondage gear had been turned against him by a woman who wielded humiliation like a surgeon's scalpel.

Every movement sent lightning through his shoulders, muscles screaming from being wrenched into positions they were never meant to hold. The chair's ergonomic design, so carefully engineered for executive comfort during long board meetings, had become an instrument of exquisite torture when horizontal.

He tried to work some saliva around the gag, but his mouth had gone desert dry. The rubber ball felt enormous, forcing his jaw into an ache that radiated into his temples. He'd worn the same gag dozens of times during his carefully orchestrated encounters, but always as the one in control. Always as the man holding the key.

The irony wasn't lost on him. The woman from Riverton had used his own predilections to reduce him to this—a powerful man rendered helpless by the very instruments of control he'd used to dominate others.

A knock at the door shattered the suffocating quiet.

Harlan's entire body seized with desperate hope. Morrison. Finally. His security chief had probably finished dropping off the girl—Sandra? Sarah? He'd already forgotten her name—and returned to find his principal missing from the restaurant downstairs. Standard protocol would bring him here to investigate.

He tried to call out, but the gag reduced his voice to a strangled "Mmmmph!" The sound was pathetic, barely human.

Silence stretched like a held breath. Then another knock, harder this time, urgent.

"Sir? You in there?"

Morrison's voice carried the tension of a professional who'd found something wrong with his carefully ordered world. Harlan had been paying the man for six years to anticipate problems, neutralize threats, and maintain the illusion that powerful men were untouchable. Tonight, Morrison's most basic responsibility—keeping his principal safe—had failed spectacularly.

Harlan thrashed against the restraints, the chair legs scraping against expensive carpet. His muffled shouts came out as desperate groans, each one burning his throat.

Get in here, you incompetent—

"Sir, I'm coming in."

The electronic lock clicked with the soft authority of a keycard override—Morrison had insisted on backup access to every location Harlan frequented, standard security protocol for a man who made enemies as easily as he made campaign contributions. The door swung open with a whisper of well-oiled hinges.

Morrison stepped through and froze.

For a moment that stretched like molten glass, the security man stood in the threshold, his mouth agape, as though struggling to process the scene before him. Morrison had served two tours in Afghanistan before transitioning to private security. He'd seen IED explosions, firefights, the aftermath of suicide bombings. But the look on his face told Harlan that nothing in his military experience had prepared him for this.

His boss—United States Congressman William Harlan, Chairman of the House Subcommittee on Cybersecurity, a man who shaped national defense policy—lay on his side like a discarded mannequin. Naked and cuffed to an overturned office chair with what was obviously high-end bondage equipment.

"What the ..." Morrison's voice trailed off as his training warred with disbelief.

Harlan's eyes bulged with the strain of trying to communicate through humiliation and rubber. He jerked his head violently toward the bed—the universal gesture for *stop gawking and help me, you idiot.*

Morrison crossed the room in three efficient strides, grabbed the chair's arms, and hauled it upright with the kind of controlled strength that came from years of moving heavy equipment under fire.

Once vertical, Morrison reached for the gag without hesitation. No questions. No commentary. The mark of a professional who understood that some situations required action first and understanding later. One of the reasons Harlan kept him around.

"That bitch," he muttered as the red rubber ball came free, trailing strings of saliva like some obscene birth.

"The key!" Harlan's voice was hoarse from thirty minutes of muffled screaming. "On the bed. Find the key!"

Morrison turned toward the king-size bed and paused. The duvet looked like a high-end sex shop had exploded across it. He pushed aside the implements without comment, searching through silk sheets.

The key glinted under a leather harness that looked like it belonged on a very expensive horse. Morrison grabbed it and unlocked the cuffs with the same efficiency he brought to everything else. No wasted motion. No unnecessary drama.

Harlan's arms dropped like dead weight, circulation screaming back to life in a symphony of needles and fire. He rolled his shoulders, trying to work feeling back into limbs that had been twisted at unnatural angles for too long.

"What happened?" Morrison asked, already moving to gather Harlan's scattered clothes from various locations around the room. The congressman's suit jacket had ended up draped over a lampshade. His pants were crumpled beside the bathroom door. His tie hung from the headboard like a silk noose.

"Maybe if you'd done your job," Harlan snarled, snatching his pants from Morrison's hands, "some random woman wouldn't have been able to waltz in here."

Morrison straightened, his face carefully neutral. "A woman did this?"

Harlan bit back the rage threatening to explode from his chest. Morrison had been following orders—driving the girl home as instructed, maintaining the careful choreography that kept Harlan's extracurricular activities separate from his public image. This wasn't entirely the security man's fault.

Just mostly.

"Get out," Harlan said, pulling on his shirt with hands that shook from more than just restored circulation. "Wait in the hall."

Morrison hesitated for exactly one second then nodded and headed for the door.

"Sir—" he began.

"Out." The word came out flat.

The door clicked shut.

Harlan finished dressing with movements sharp as broken glass, each gesture a small violence against the memory of the past hour. His wrists bore angry red marks where the leather had cut into flesh. He'd been gifted with a stigma of his own perverted appetites turned against him. His jaw ached from the gag; muscles cramped from being forced open longer than anatomy intended.

But worse than the physical discomfort was the memory of her eyes. She'd been so calm and completely in control while he sat there exposed and helpless. She'd taken photographs. Evidence. Insurance that would guarantee his compliance or destroy him if he tried to renege on their deal. The images existed somewhere out there in the digital ether, waiting to surface at the worst possible moment.

He grabbed his phone from the charger on the nightstand, a small island of normalcy amid the wreckage of his evening. His contacts list was a who's who of Washington power brokers, but there was only one number that mattered now.

The contact was labeled simply "K."

Three rings. Then a voice crackled.

"It's late." David Kern didn't sound surprised by the call. Men in their line of work learned to expect the unexpected at all hours.

"We have a problem." Harlan kept his voice level, professional, the tone he used in classified briefings when discussing threats to national security.

"Define problem."

Harlan took a breath, choosing his words. A man who understood that careers could be destroyed by careless language. "The woman from Riverton. She was here. Tonight."

The silence on the other end stretched long enough for Harlan to count his heartbeats. When Kern spoke again, his voice had shifted into a different register—the cold focus of a predator who'd just caught a scent.

"Explain."

"She ... interrogated me. About you. About AeroSight." Harlan couldn't bring himself to describe the specifics—the chrome dildo, the bondage gear, the photographs that could end his career in a single news cycle. Some humiliations were too complete to share, even with an ally. "I sent her your way."

"You did what?"

The three words carried enough menace to freeze blood. Harlan pressed on, knowing that retreat would only make things worse.

"I told her about Carter. About tomorrow morning."

When Kern finally spoke, each word was precise as a scalpel cut. "You told a hostile operator about a sensitive operation. Have you completely lost your mind?"

"Listen—"

"What if she warns Carter? What if she goes to the press? What if she's recording this conversation right now?" Kern's voice carried that familiar calculating edge. "What if—"

"She won't." Harlan cut him off before the spiral of paranoia could gain momentum. "If she wanted to go public about Riverton, she would have already. Every major news outlet would be running the story. She doesn't want exposure. She wants revenge. She's a blade, not a megaphone."

More silence. Harlan could practically hear Kern's mind working, calculating angles and probabilities, how quickly he could eliminate a liability. David Kern hadn't survived in the shadow world by making emotional decisions or allowing sentiment to cloud his judgment.

"Fine," Kern said, his voice returning to its normal register of controlled menace. "I'll kill two birds with one stone."

"Make sure it's clean. We don't need anyone else poking around." Harlan glanced toward the bed, where the evidence of his evening still lay scattered across the silk. "This thing has to stay contained."

"I know my business, Congressman."

"And Kern?" Harlan's voice dropped to barely above a whisper.

"When you deal with her, make sure you get her phone. Destroy it. Completely."

"When I erase someone, nothing's left."

The line went dead.

Harlan stood in the empty hotel room, fully dressed but feeling more naked than when he'd been bound and gagged on the floor. His wrists throbbed with each heartbeat. His dignity lay in pieces around him like the scattered implements of his own destruction.

The room felt contaminated now, poisoned by memories that would never fully fade. Every surface held evidence of his humiliation—the chair where he'd been bound, the bed where his secrets lay exposed, the carpet that had pressed against his cheek while he silently begged for rescue.

After gathering all of his expensive toys back into the briefcase, he opened the door to find Morrison leaning against the hallway wall with patient stillness. He straightened as Harlan emerged, his face a carefully maintained mask of professional neutrality.

"We're leaving," Harlan said.

"Yes, sir. The car's—"

"And Morrison?" Harlan's voice dropped to barely above a whisper, carrying the weight of unspoken threats. "This never happened. Ever. Are we clear?"

Morrison's face remained stone, but something flickered behind his eyes—recognition, perhaps, of the implicit bargain. Silence for continued employment. Discretion for security.

"What never happened, sir?"

"Good man."

They walked to the elevator in silence. Harlan kept his chin up, his stride confident, every movement calculated to project the image of a man in complete control. But inside, her words echoed like a curse:

Next time, no safe word.

There wouldn't be a next time. Kern would make sure of that. By tomorrow night, Hatch would be just another casualty in a war she never should have joined—another problem solved with the kind of permanent efficiency that men like Kern specialized in.

The elevator doors closed on the ninth floor, sealing away the last physical evidence of the night's humiliation. But Harlan knew that some stains didn't wash out. Some moments branded themselves into memory, surfacing at the worst times like psychological shrapnel.

He'd been broken by a woman with a scar and a chrome-plated sex toy.

That kind of shame didn't fade. It metastasized, spreading through the psyche like cancer until it consumed everything healthy and normal. It would color every interaction, poison every moment of apparent triumph, whisper reminders of weakness in the spaces between sleeping and waking.

The lobby was tomb-quiet when they exited, the kind of expensive silence that came from thick carpet and sound-insulated walls. The night clerk didn't look up from his computer screen—discretion was a premium service at establishments like The Whitmore, where powerful men came to conduct business that couldn't survive in daylight.

Morrison led the way to the car with his usual professionalism, maintaining the careful fiction that nothing had changed between them. But he had seen. They both knew it. The dynamic between principal and protector had shifted in ways that would never fully return to normal.

The black government sedan waited under the hotel's porte-cochère like a faithful hound. Morrison held the door, then circled to the driver's seat with movements that betrayed nothing of what he'd witnessed upstairs. But Harlan caught him glancing in the rearview mirror—not at traffic, but at his principal, reassessing threat levels and probability matrices in light of new information.

And somewhere out there in the dark, the woman from Riverton was driving toward a mountain rest stop, unaware that she'd just signed her own death warrant. She thought she was clever, thought she held the advantage because she'd managed to humiliate a congressman and extract information about AeroSight's operations.

She had no idea what kind of enemy she'd made.

Kern didn't make threats. He made bodies disappear. He made

problems vanish so completely that people forgot they'd ever existed in the first place.

By dawn, he'd make good on that promise.

The sedan pulled into D.C. traffic, joining the river of power and ambition that flowed through the capital city even at midnight. Behind them, The Whitmore Hotel stood like a monument to discretion and buried secrets.

Tomorrow would bring a new crisis, a new problem to solve. But tonight's humiliation would never fully heal.

Some wounds were meant to fester.

NINE

THE MOUNTAIN ROADS AT NIGHT WERE A DIFFERENT BEAST entirely. No traffic to follow, no sun to soften the jagged edges where asphalt met wilderness. Just headlights carving tunnels through absolute darkness and the steady thrum of tires on pavement that hadn't seen maintenance funding since the previous administration.

Hatch downshifted as the grade steepened, her Jeep's engine growling with the satisfaction. The road twisted through gaps in the ridge line like a snake following some ancient path of least resistance, each curve revealing nothing but more darkness ahead.

She checked the dashboard clock, nearly 2AM. The green digits glowed with electronic certainty in the instrument cluster, marking time that felt both endless and insufficient. She'd put several hours and plenty of mountain road between herself and Congressman Harlan's depths of humiliation. By now Morrison would have found him, freed him from his chrome-plated shame, probably driven him home to his Georgetown townhouse where he'd scrub himself raw trying to wash off the memory.

Let him scrub. Some stains went deeper than skin, penetrating all the way down to the soul where they festered and spread like psychological gangrene.

The radio crackled with static—too far from any decent transmitter, too deep in the mountains for clear reception. Country music from West Virginia. A late-night call-in show from somewhere in Tennessee where insomniacs shared their theories about everything wrong with the modern world.

Mile marker 45 slid past in her peripheral vision, reflective numbers catching her headlights for an instant before disappearing back into darkness. Then 46, the sign crooked as if it had been knocked askew by a careless snowplow and never straightened. Hatch began to slow, scanning the tree line with methodical attention.

She took the exit at mile marker 47, barely visible beneath years of weather and deliberate neglect. The metal sign was pocked with what looked like bullet holes, probably the work of locals using it for target practice. Rust bloomed around the edges like cancer, and someone had spray-painted what might have been initials across the bottom in faded blue letters.

The northbound rest area sat just beyond the marker, a pull-off that was little more than a widening in the road with a couple of picnic tables and an information board about local wildlife that nobody ever read. No facilities, no amenities, just a place where travelers could stop to stretch their legs. Hatch pulled off to do just that.

She killed the engine. Silence rushed in like water filling a vacuum. No wind stirring the pine branches. Just the tick of cooling metal and the sound of her own breathing, loud in the enclosed space of the cab.

Hatch stepped out of the Jeep. She breathed in the fresh mountain air. The Blue Ridge meant forty-degree nights even when the days were starting to usher in spring. Her breath misted as she walked the perimeter of the rest area, noting sight lines, cover positions, escape routes. If things broke bad, it was always good to have a fallback point.

The burner phone buzzed against her hip, the vibration sharp and insistent in the mountain quiet. She'd picked up the smartphone three towns back—paid for with cash, activated with false information, the kind of disposable technology that would become untraceable the moment she threw it in a dumpster. Hatch pulled it out and saw

Banyan's name on the display, because of course. The man had a sixth sense for when she was neck-deep in something that could go sideways, some kind of psychological radar that activated whenever she started making decisions that rational people would question.

The text was brief, characteristic of his dry humor: *Tell me you're not in over your head.*

Hatch's thumb hovered over the keyboard, the cursor blinking with electronic patience. She could tell him everything—Harlan's kinky humiliation, the briefcase full of sex toys that had become an impromptu interrogation toolkit, the whistleblower marked for death by men who viewed murder as just another business expense. Banyan would want to help. Would probably insist on it, offering resources and backup and technological support that could tip the scales in her favor.

Which was exactly why she deleted the draft without sending it.

The phone went back in her pocket unanswered. Banyan would understand eventually. Or he wouldn't. Either way, he'd stay safe, which was all that mattered. The people she cared about had a habit of becoming casualties in wars they'd never signed up for.

Her personal phone showed a missed call from her mother, the notification glowing softly in the darkness. No voicemail, but none was needed. Hatch knew what the call was about. Daphne's tenth birthday party was fast approaching. She'd made a promise to the little girl whose innocence brought Hatch into a world she rarely got to experience.

Hatch had promised to be there. Had every intention of keeping that promise, assuming she survived the next twenty-four hours. The thought of disappointing Daphne was almost more motivation than justice itself.

But first, she had to make sure a scientist she'd never met lived to see another sunrise.

Nothing good came from sitting in the dark, waiting for trouble to find you. Every minute spent in a static position was a minute the enemy could use to improve their positioning, gather intelligence, or simply work up the nerve to pull triggers. Movement was life, even when it felt like running toward danger instead of away from it.

Hatch started the engine and pulled back onto the mountain highway, headlights once again pushing back the darkness. Five miles down the grade, a flickering neon sign materialized from the void like a beacon calling ships to harbor. Pete's Diner—Home of the Bottomless Cup. The promise of hot coffee and human contact, even if temporary.

This was where Carter would come at dawn. Where Kern's people would be waiting with whatever trap they'd constructed. Where everything would converge in approximately five hours.

The parking lot was half-full of eighteen-wheelers, their running lights creating constellations in the darkness. Diesel engines idled with the deep, throaty rumble that spoke of power held in reserve, ready to haul cargo across the continental United States on highways that never slept.

Hatch found a spot in the far corner, backing her Jeep in. Quick exits sometimes meant the difference between breathing and bleeding out. Clear view of the entrance, unobstructed line to the highway, no vehicles that could box her in. Old habits from a different life, but habits that had kept her alive when other people's luck ran out.

Inside, Pete's Diner was exactly what central casting would have ordered for a late-night truck stop. Cracked vinyl booths held together by duct tape and stubbornness, yellowed walls decorated with faded Route 66 memorabilia that probably predated the interstate highway system. The smell hit her like a warm slap—coffee strong enough to wake the dead mixing with bacon grease, cigarette smoke, and industrial floor cleaner that suggested someone still cared about basic hygiene despite the dated décor.

A handful of truckers hunched over the counter like supplicants at an altar, nursing ceramic mugs that looked like they'd survived decades of refills. Their conversation was a low murmur punctuated by the occasional laugh, the easy camaraderie of men who spent their lives on the road and understood that diners like Pete's were islands of civilization in an ocean of darkness.

"Anywhere you like, hon," the waitress called out without looking up from the coffee pot she was refilling. Beneath a forced, tired smile, the name tag reading "Darlene" in letters that had faded to match her dyed blonde hair. The kind of woman who'd probably been working nights since Hatch was in diapers, collecting stories and tips in equal measure.

Hatch chose a booth that gave her sight lines to both exits and a window view of the parking lot. The cracked vinyl sighed as she sat, complaining about its age and the accumulated weight of thousands of travelers who'd stopped here over the decades. The table was scarred with cigarette burns and coffee rings but wiped clean with the kind of thoroughness that spoke to professional pride.

Darlene appeared as if summoned, pot already in hand, the practiced efficiency of a woman who could read customer needs from across the room. "Coffee?"

"Please. And breakfast."

"All day, every day, sugar. What'll it be?"

"Eggs over easy, wheat toast, hash browns."

"Coming right up. You want that coffee unleaded or high-test?"

"High-test. It's going to be a long night."

Darlene poured without comment, the stream black as motor oil and probably twice as strong.

The coffee was exactly what Hatch needed—bitter enough to cut through exhaustion, strong enough to restart a dead engine. She cradled the mug between her palms, letting the heat seep into fingers that had gone cold during the mountain drive, and settled in to watch the room.

One of the truckers at the counter caught her attention, not because he triggered any threat assessment but because of the sheer incongruity he presented. Easily six-foot-five, built like he bench-pressed engine blocks for recreation, hands that could palm basketballs or crush beer cans with casual pressure. The kind of man you'd expect to find in a honky-tonk parking lot settling disputes with violence.

But cradled in his massive lap sat the tiniest dog Hatch had ever seen—some kind of Chihuahua mix that couldn't have weighed more than five pounds soaking wet. The little creature wore a miniature hoodie that read "Bad to the Bone" in glittery letters, the rhinestones catching the diner's fluorescent lights like tiny stars.

The giant was sharing his breakfast with the dog, carefully spooning small bites of scrambled eggs and offering them to the eager mouth. His movements were gentle, precise, the kind of tenderness usually reserved for newborn babies or wounded birds. The little dog accepted each offering with the regal dignity of royalty being served by devoted servants.

"Darlene, darlin', what's the damage?" the trucker asked, pulling out a wallet that looked like it had seen more miles than most people's cars.

"Same as always, Raff. Though I should charge extra for feeding that spoiled mutt."

"Princess Mayhem isn't spoiled," Raff protested with mock indignation, scratching behind the dog's ears and causing a contented whine that sounded like a tiny motor. "She's selectively appreciated. There's a difference."

"If you say so. Mind if I ask what a dog that size needs with a name like Princess Mayhem?"

Raff's grin could have powered the diner's neon sign. "You ever seen her when someone tries to take her favorite squeaky toy? Little thing's got more fight per pound than most prizefighters. Size ain't everything, you know."

"I'll take your word for it." Darlene's smile was genuine, the kind that came from years of watching the peculiar bonds that formed between lonely people and their chosen family. "You catching some rack time in the lot?"

"Got to be in Richmond by noon, but these old bones need rest." He stood carefully, cradling the dog like precious cargo. "Mind if I park out back? Princess gets nervous with too much truck traffic."

"You know you don't have to ask."

"Mama always said, 'Better to ask than assume.'" He touched the brim of his battered Pittsburgh Steelers cap in a gesture that belonged to a more courteous era. "Plus, gives me an excuse to see your pretty face one more time."

"Flirt. Get out of here before I charge you double."

Raff chuckled and left money on the counter with what looked like a generous tip, then headed for the exit with the careful gait of a man who'd spent decades climbing in and out of truck cabs. As he walked, he hummed something low and country—Waylon Jennings maybe, "Mama Tried"—the tune mixing with Princess Mayhem's contented whimpering as she settled deeper into his arms.

Hatch watched him lumber toward the door, cataloging details: the slight favor he showed his left knee, probably an old injury that ached before weather changes; the way he moved his shoulders, suggesting lower back problems from too many years hunched over a steering wheel; the unconscious scan he gave the parking lot before stepping outside, the residual awareness of someone who'd learned that truck stops could be dangerous places for the unwary.

Through the window, she tracked him to his rig—a blue Peterbilt with a desert sunrise mural painted on the cab door. Cactuses and mesas rendered in brilliant oranges and reds, a sun that looked like it was setting the world on fire. The artwork was professional quality, the kind of custom paint job that truckers commissioned when their rigs became more than just transportation—when they became homes, identities, statements about who they were and where they'd been.

Hard to miss, which made it perfect for remembering later if needed. In Hatch's experience, witnesses came in two varieties: those who noticed everything and those who noticed nothing. The trick was figuring out which kind you were dealing with before you needed their testimony.

"Here you go, hon." Darlene materialized beside the table with a plate that looked like it belonged in a magazine advertisement for authentic American cooking. "Anything else?"

"Actually, yeah. Is there a motel nearby? Need to grab a few hours before dawn."

"Hilltop Inn, couple miles west. Can't miss it—big sign with half the letters burned out. It's not the Ritz, but the sheets are clean and the doors lock solid."

"Sounds perfect."

"You traveling alone?" The question came with casual concern.

Hatch nodded. "For now."

Darlene nodded back, understanding the boundaries of truck stop conversation. Sometimes people wanted to talk, to share their stories with a sympathetic stranger who'd forget their faces by morning. Sometimes they just wanted food and coffee and the blessing of anonymity.

Hatch ate methodically, fueling rather than enjoying, though she had to admit the food was better than expected. The eggs were actually over easy instead of the rubber discs most diners served. The hash browns had been cooked in honest grease until they achieved the perfect balance of crispy exterior and fluffy interior. The wheat toast was thick-cut and golden, the kind that required actual chewing.

Normal food for a deeply abnormal night.

She'd saved towns before—stopped men like Kern who viewed human casualties as acceptable costs of doing business. But the mathematics of violence never changed. There was always a price. Always someone who didn't make it home to kiss their spouse goodnight or read bedtime stories to children who believed their parents were invincible.

The weight of that accumulated debt pressed against her chest, familiar as an old scar that ached before storms. Every life she'd saved had cost someone else their life. Every victory had come with a bill that someone else had to pay. The ledger never balanced, just shifted the burden from one column to another.

She checked the time again—3:45 AM. Still hours before Carter's meeting, before whatever trap Kern had designed would spring shut. Before she stepped into the middle of it all with nothing but skill and stubbornness and a lifelong code.

The diner had grown quieter as the night deepened. Just Hatch and one remaining trucker who looked like he was sleeping upright over his coffee, head nodding in the rhythm of a man fighting exhaustion and losing. Darlene wiped down tables with the mechanical movements of someone who could perform this job in her sleep—and probably sometimes did.

Hatch left cash on the table with a decent tip—enough to be remembered as generous but not so much as to be memorable for the wrong reasons. Outside, the night had turned colder, the mountain air carrying the promise of frost. Her breath misted in the air as she walked to her Jeep.

In the back of the lot, she could see Raff's Peterbilt among the other rigs, dark now except for a small night light visible through the cab window. Man and dog, catching what rest they could before the next leg of their journey across America's highway system. There was something comforting about the image—simple contentment in the face of complexity, loyalty that didn't require explanation or justification.

The Hilltop Inn was exactly as advertised—a single-story motor lodge that had seen better decades, half its neon sign dark with burned-out tubes, the other half flickering like it was sending distress signals to passing aircraft. But the office light was on, and that was all she needed. The building had the weathered look of a place that had survived the transition from state roads to the interstate era, adapting without thriving.

The night clerk barely looked up from his phone as he slid a key across the counter—not a keycard, but an actual metal key attached to a plastic fob shaped like a miniature mountain. Room 12. Ground floor, end unit. Perfect for quick exits if the situation deteriorated.

Hatch did a walk-around first, checking sight lines and noting potential problems: the dumpster that could provide cover but also concealment for hostiles; the chain link fence that could be vaulted but might snag clothing or equipment; the parking lot layout that offered multiple escape routes but also multiple avenues of approach for unwanted visitors.

The door was solid enough—metal frame, deadbolt that looked like it had been installed sometime in the current century. She tested the window and found it painted shut years ago, probably as much from institutional neglect as security considerations. One way in, one way out. Not ideal from a tactical standpoint, but workable if you understood the limitations.

Inside, she wedged a chair under the doorknob—a field expedient security measure that wouldn't stop a determined assault but would buy precious seconds of warning. She set her phone alarm for 6 AM, then sat on the bed that smelled like industrial detergent and the accumulated dreams of a thousand anonymous travelers.

Sleep never came easy on nights like this, when violence waited just beyond the horizon like a storm gathering strength. Not when her mind insisted on running through contingencies, calculating odds, reviewing the thousand things that could go wrong and the dozen things that might go right.

But she'd learned to rest without sleeping, to let her body recover while her mind stayed sharp and alert. Rest was ammunition, and she'd need every round.

The calm before the storm was always the worst part. That feeling of inevitability, of forces converging beyond her control, of violence gathering like thunderclouds on the horizon. She'd felt it before—in Afghanistan before the suicide bombing that had left her scarred in ways both visible and hidden. In Riverton before everything had gone to hell and good people died because she'd been a step too slow, a thought too late.

Morning would come. But tonight, she had a bed, and a locked door and a few hours to gather her strength before stepping once more into the path of dangerous men who thought they owned the world.

Let them think it.

She'd spent a career proving them wrong, one bullet at a time.

TEN

MARCUS THORNE STOOD UNDER A FLICKERING PARKING lot light, phone pressed to his ear, watching moths dance their death spiral around the dying fluorescent bulb. The insects circled with mindless determination, drawn to the harsh white glow like pilgrims to a false prophet, each pass bringing them closer to the inevitable collision that would end their brief existence.

The Roadway Inn sprawled behind him in the Virginia darkness—a testament to the interstate highway system's ability to spawn identical concrete boxes across the American landscape. Twenty miles from the target location, close enough to respond when the time came, far enough to avoid notice from locals or law enforcement who might wonder why so many hard-looking men had appeared in their quiet mountain community.

Just another forgettable motel on a forgettable stretch of highway. The kind of place where cash transactions went unquestioned and security cameras had been broken for longer than anyone could remember.

David Kern's voice came through the encrypted satellite phone, cold and precise as a surgical blade cutting through diseased tissue. "Status."

"All assets in position." Thorne kept his own voice level, professional, drained of any emotion that might suggest this was anything more than another day at the office. Eight years of private military work had taught him that clients like Kern valued efficiency over enthusiasm, results over rhetoric. "Team One ready for intercept at the primary location. Team Two has eyes on the secondary."

"Walk me through it."

Thorne shifted, moving away from the light and into the shadow cast by his black Suburban. Old habits from Afghanistan, where standing silhouetted against illumination was an invitation for snipers to practice their craft.

"Simple and clean. Garcia and Mitchell approach Carter at the diner. Mitchell goes inside, makes friendly contact—maybe flash federal credentials, DHS or FBI, whatever sells best. Tell him there's been a credible threat against his family, we need to move him somewhere secure for debriefing."

He could picture it unfolding with the smooth efficiency of a well-rehearsed play. Carter would be nervous already, jumping at shadows, perfect psychological setup for a rescue that wasn't a rescue at all.

"Garcia stays with the sedan, engine running, ready for immediate extraction. Our reconnaissance confirms the diner has no working exterior cameras—management's been putting off the repair for months. Once Mitchell convinces Carter to step outside, they're gone in under sixty seconds."

Thorne shifted again, checking his watch. "They move him to a secondary location away from any potential witnesses, retrieve the materials, and arrange an accident. Mountain roads, early morning fog, plenty of options. Drunk driver crosses the center line, maybe. Or mechanical failure on a steep grade. These old mountain highways claim lives every month."

"And the family?"

"Insurance policy only. Kowalski and I maintain surveillance on the cabin—close enough to respond if needed, far enough to stay invisible. If Carter needs additional motivation to cooperate, we're already in position to leverage the wife and kid. But that's a last resort. Much cleaner if it's just him."

"Good." A pause on Kern's end, filled with the sound of ice clinking against crystal. Probably aged whiskey, something expensive enough to match the man's taste for quality tools and permanent solutions. "There's been a development."

Thorne's jaw tightened. In his line of work, developments were like cancer—they metastasized quickly and usually killed the host. Complications meant variables, variables meant chaos, and chaos got good operators killed by people who should have been easy targets.

"The woman from Riverton," Kern said. "She's been alerted to the situation."

"How?" The question came out sharper than Thorne intended, but Kern's revelation had just doubled the complexity of an operation that was supposed to be routine asset recovery.

"Irrelevant. What matters is she'll likely attempt to interfere. I want her handled."

Thorne glanced across the parking lot at his team. Garcia leaned against a dark sedan, cigarette glowing between his fingers like a tiny orange beacon in the darkness. The man had picked up the smoking habit in Syria and never managed to shake it, despite Thorne repeatedly warning him about operational security and the visibility of burning tobacco from a thousand meters away.

Mitchell stood beside the sedan, checking his gear. Overlooked details got people killed. Kowalski waited by Thorne's SUV.

"Parameters?" Thorne asked.

"Complete erasure," Kern said, his voice carrying an edge. "No body, no trace, no questions. She cost me considerably in Texas. That debt needs settling."

"Understood. Priority?"

"Carter is primary. The evidence must be secured—that thumb drive contains enough information to bring down everything we've built. But the woman..." Kern's voice dropped a degree, taking on the tone of someone who'd made a careful study of a particular enemy. "She walked through Riverton like it was a training exercise. Neutralized a full tactical team without breaking a sweat. Don't underestimate her."

"We won't."

"I expect confirmation by sunrise. Both problems resolved, both threats eliminated."

The line went dead without farewell, leaving only the soft hiss of static and the expectation of results. Kern wasn't the type for pleasantries or encouragement. He hired professionals, gave them clear objectives, and expected those objectives to be met regardless of complications or casualties.

Thorne pocketed the phone and walked across the parking lot toward Garcia. The night carried the sharp edge of coming winter, mountain air that promised frost before dawn.

"Kill that cigarette," he said as he approached. "We're moving in two hours."

Garcia took a long drag, exhaled slowly through his nose like a dragon savoring its own fire. "These things'll kill me anyway. Figure I might as well enjoy the process."

"Not if you keep lighting up on operations. That cherry's visible at three hundred meters through night vision. Makes you a priority target for anyone with a scope and bad intentions."

"You sound like my ex-wife." Garcia flicked the butt into a puddle where it hissed like an angry snake and went dark. "Always nagging about something."

Mitchell's voice crackled through their earpieces from the van\. "Which ex-wife? You've got what, three now?"

"Funny." Garcia's grin was visible in the parking lot's harsh lighting. "We good to go, or are we having a sensitivity training session?"

"Change of plans." Thorne kept his voice level but knew Garcia caught the shift in tone immediately. Years of working together had taught them to read each other's moods like weather patterns. "Got a secondary target. The woman from Riverton."

Garcia's expression sobered. They'd all heard the stories filtering through the private military community—half of Talon's B-team taken apart by a single operator. Power grids restored, hostages rescued, their entire operation burned to the ground by someone who moved through tactical situations like a force of nature.

"She's here? In the area?"

"Will be. Boss wants her gone. Permanently."

"Shit." Garcia's hand moved to check his sidearm. "That's going to change the whole dynamic."

"Only if we let it." Thorne keyed his radio, switching to the encrypted channel that would connect them once they reached their positions. "Remember, Garcia and Mitchell handle the primary target. Kowalski and I maintain overwatch on the family. Nobody touches the civilians unless I give explicit authorization. We're not in the business of killing women and children unless absolutely necessary."

Mitchell's voice came back steady and professional. "Copy that."

Thorne did a mental inventory of available resources. Four operators, all with extensive combat experience. Two vehicles—the SUV and the surveillance van, both equipped with communication gear and enough firepower to handle significant resistance. Body armor, night vision, suppressed weapons, medical supplies, extraction equipment.

Against one scientist carrying stolen data and one woman with a dangerous reputation. Should be sufficient force to handle any contingency.

But Thorne had been in this business long enough to know that simple operations had a way of going sideways when you added variables like Hatch to the equation. Variables that turned routine asset recovery into the kind of cluster that made front-page news and congressional investigations.

"Load up," he told Garcia. "I want weapons checked, routes memorized, contingencies reviewed. Communication protocols confirmed. If this goes smooth and quick, we're drinking beer by lunch and counting our money."

"And if it doesn't go smooth?"

Thorne's smile was humorless, the expression of a man who'd seen too many operations turn into disasters when overconfidence met unexpected resistance. "Then we earn our hazard pay the hard way."

Garcia and Mitchell loaded their gear into the sedan while Thorne and Kowalski prepared the SUV for the drive to the cabin.

Body armor rated for rifle rounds. Suppressed weapons with enough ammunition to fight a small war. Flex cuffs for prisoner handling. Trauma kits for when things went wrong and people started bleeding. Electronic surveillance equipment. False identification. Cash in various denominations. The accumulated hardware of men who solved problems in countries where the rule of law was more suggestion than requirement.

Garcia and Mitchell would head directly to the diner, arriving early enough to conduct final reconnaissance and position themselves for the intercept. Thorne and Kowalski would take the mountain roads to the cabin, establishing overwatch positions in case family leverage became necessary.

Thorne settled into the driver's seat of the SUV as Kowalski climbed in beside him. Carter's meeting was scheduled for seven—two hours to reach the cabin, establish surveillance positions, and coordinate with the other team.

"You really think she'll show?" Kowalski asked, adjusting his earpiece and checking the radio frequency.

"Kern's many things, but paranoid isn't one of them." Thorne started the engine, watching Garcia and Mitchell pull out in the sedan ahead of them. "He's also not the type to waste resources on imaginary problems. If he says she's coming, she's coming."

"So what's the play if she shows?"

"Garcia and Mitchell handle it at the diner. Fast and hard. No conversation, no negotiation, no attempts at capture or interrogation. They put her down immediately with maximum force and move on to the primary objective." Thorne's voice carried the flat certainty of someone who'd made similar calculations countless times before. "Lead and physics solve a lot of problems."

Kowalski nodded, but Thorne could see him running the numbers in his head. Two professionals with military training and superior equipment versus one woman, regardless of her reputation. The mathematics should favor them heavily.

Should being the operative word.

The sky was beginning to lighten in the east, purple bleeding into gray as dawn approached with the inevitability of an execution. Soon the mountains would emerge from darkness like sleeping giants awakening to judge the actions of smaller creatures. In a few hours, it would all be over—Carter silenced, evidence secured, the woman from Riverton reduced to a statistic that would never appear in any official report.

ELEVEN

HATCH OPENED HER EYES FIVE MINUTES BEFORE HER 6AM alarm sounded. Her previous life had gifted her with the precision of an internal chronometer that had been calibrated by years of operations where being late meant being dead. Her body had long ago learned to keep its own time, especially when violence waited on the horizon like a storm that could be felt through her bones before the first drops fell. No way that Harlan hadn't tipped off Kern. Her plan had always been to draw the head of AeroSight into the light. And if that meant putting herself in harm's way to do it then so be it.

The motel room was still dark, dawn just a promise bleeding through the thin curtains that had seen better decades. Outside, she could hear the soft percussion of dew dripping from the eaves and the distant hum of early morning traffic beginning to build on the interstate. The world stirring to life while she prepared for death.

She moved through her morning routine with military economy—splash of cold water on the face that shocked her fully awake, quick brush of teeth with the travel toothbrush she'd grabbed from a gas station.

The morning run would have to wait. Today required different preparations.

Hatch left the room key on the unmanned front desk—a small courtesy that would delay questions when housekeeping found the empty room later—and stepped into the pre-dawn chill. Springtime in the mountains held onto winter's edge, offering air crisp enough to sting her lungs. The parking lot was tomb-quiet except for the rustle of wind through dying leaves.

The Jeep waited for her like a patient dog, faithful and reliable despite its collection of dents and rust spots. But before climbing in, she knelt by the rear wheel well, reaching her fingers inside to find the concealed latch, invisible unless you knew exactly where to look.

The compartment opened with a soft click that sounded loud in the morning quiet. A subcompact Glock rested in its holster.

She press-checked it from habit—not because she doubted it was ready, but because the ritual of verification had saved her life more than once. The weight of it settled against her spine as she secured it in the holster, familiar as an old friend's handshake, comforting as a prayer in a language only she spoke.

The drive to Pete's Diner took twelve minutes through mountain roads that twisted between hills like the spine of some sleeping giant. The roads were empty except for the occasional long hauler heading for morning deliveries, their running lights creating brief constellations in her rearview mirror before disappearing around curves that led to destinations she'd never see.

She kept the radio off, windows cracked, letting the cold air flow through the cab and sharpen her focus to a diamond point. Mile marker 47 slid past in her peripheral vision, and she noted the rest stop beyond it—empty picnic tables wearing their morning dew like silver armor, the information board about local wildlife.

Pete's Diner materialized from the dawn gloom like a ship emerging from fog, its neon sign still fighting its losing battle against the rising sun. The parking lot held more vehicles now than it had during her earlier visit.

In the far corner, Raff's Peterbilt still idled, exhaust rising from its stacks in lazy spirals that suggested the big man was awake but not ready to face the world yet. Probably sharing his breakfast with

Princess Mayhem and humming country songs that belonged to a simpler time.

Hatch parked with clear sight lines to the entrance and both exits. She pulled out the burner and scrolled to the saved article she'd found during her research, the digital breadcrumbs that had led her to understand what Samuel Carter really was.

Dr. Samuel Carter's face filled the small screen, frozen in a moment of uncomfortable formality. The photo was from a Georgetown University awards banquet two years ago, back when his research was still theoretical and his conscience was still clear. He looked uncomfortable in his tuxedo and wore a forced smile that suggested he'd rather be anywhere else.

The article praised his "groundbreaking work in induced seismic stress relief"—a clinical phrase that made controlled earthquakes sound like physical therapy for mountains. The science was elegant in its simplicity: create small, controlled fractures along fault lines to relieve pressure gradually instead of letting it build to catastrophic levels. It was the geological equivalent of controlled burns in forest management, preventing the big disasters by managing the small ones.

She read the key passage again, the words that explained how a man's life work could be perverted into something monstrous: *Dr. Carter's theories have attracted significant interest from DARPA, the Department of Energy, and private defense contractors. AeroSight Technologies recently acquired Dr. Carter and his research, citing "revolutionary applications in infrastructure protection."*

After that acquisition, nothing. No published papers, no conference appearances, no digital footprint at all. Samuel Carter had been swallowed by the classified world like Jonah by the whale, his theories weaponized in ways he'd probably never intended. The man who'd wanted to prevent earthquakes had instead created a weapon that could trigger them on command.

Movement in her peripheral vision pulled Hatch's attention back to the world around her. A sedan pulled into the lot—dark blue or black, hard to tell in the ambiguous morning light. Tinted windows that were just shy of the legal limit.

The vehicle crawled through the parking area like a shark sensing blood in the water, finally sliding between the two other vehicles. Nobody got out.

Hatch watched for thirty seconds, reading the body language of a vehicle at rest. Two occupants, both in front. The driver's side sat lower—bigger man, probably the muscle. They were watching, waiting, maintaining the same kind of patient surveillance that she was.

The difference was they were waiting for Carter. She was waiting for them.

Time to move. Sitting in the Jeep made her a stationary target, trapped in steel and glass if things went sideways. Better to be inside the diner, mobile, with cover and options and the ability to control the engagement on her terms.

Hatch stepped out of the Jeep, moving with the casual purpose of someone thinking about breakfast and nothing more complicated than whether to order eggs over easy or scrambled. The pistol's weight shifted against her back as she walked, a reminder that death rode with her wherever she went. She didn't look at the sedan, didn't acknowledge its existence.

The diner's warmth hit her as she pushed through the door, a wall of heated air that carried the scents of civilization. The smell of a deep fryer that had been working all night to feed truckers and insomniacs filled the air. The familiar combination of salt and fat and caffeine that formed the holy trinity of truck stop cuisine.

Darlene stood behind the counter, looking like she'd aged five years since their conversation just hours before. The overnight shift was unkind to everyone eventually, grinding down even the strongest spirits with the relentless weight of other people's needs and the fluorescent harshness of artificial lighting.

"Well, look who's back." Darlene managed a tired smile that didn't quite reach her eyes. "Food that good you had to come back for more?"

"What can I say?" Hatch replied, settling into the familiar rhythm of small talk that provided cover for more serious business. "You've ruined me for other diners."

"Honey, this place ruins everyone eventually. Counter or booth?"

"Counter's fine."

Hatch chose a stool that put her back to the wall and gave her a full view of the diner reflected in the mirror behind the coffee machines. Perfect angle to watch the front door and the parking lot without being obvious. A casual position that provided maximum tactical advantage.

Darlene poured coffee without asking. "Let me guess—you want to start with this and see where the morning takes you?"

"You're psychic."

"Nah, just been doing this too long. I'll give you a minute to decide."

The coffee was still nuclear-hot, still strong enough to wake the dead and probably strip paint if you left it sitting long enough. Hatch sipped it slowly, savoring the burn as it traveled down her throat, watching the sedan in the mirror's reflection. Still no movement. Still waiting with the patience of professionals.

She checked her phone, pretending to read the morning news or check social media. 6:43 AM. Seventeen minutes until Carter's scheduled meeting with a dead journalist. Seventeen minutes until multiple vectors of violence converged on this forgotten little diner where truckers came to fuel up and Darlene served the coffee.

Through the window, she could see Raff's dog—Princess Mayhem—pressed against the Peterbilt's window, tiny paws on the glass, watching the world with the intensity of a creature who knew it was too small to defend itself but was determined to try anyway. The little Chihuahua's eyes held an alertness that spoke to instincts honed by millions of years of evolution, an awareness that kept small things alive in a world full of larger predators.

Hatch understood the feeling better than she cared to admit.

The diner held five other customers scattered across booths and counter stools like pieces on a chess board. Two truckers at the far booth, discussing their routes over eggs and hash browns, their conversation a low murmur about weigh stations and fuel stops. An elderly man bent over a newspaper, his coffee growing cold as he worked through the crossword puzzle with the stubborn determination of someone who refused to let the world defeat him. A younger woman in scrubs, probably heading to or from a hospital shift, mainlining coffee with the desperation of the chronically exhausted.

Normal people living normal lives, unaware they were about to become extras in someone else's tragedy.

The sedan's doors remained closed, but Hatch could feel the attention emanating from within—focused and patient, the kind of watchfulness that came from men who killed for money. Professionals, then. Not local muscle or hurried amateurs, but operators who knew how to wait, how to watch, how to choose their moment for maximum effect.

Just like her.

She lifted the coffee mug again, using the motion to adjust her position slightly and confirm her weapon was still secure and accessible. When the violence came—and it would come as surely as the sunrise painting the mountains gold—she'd have maybe two seconds to react. Two seconds to decide who lived and who died in the space between heartbeats.

The sunrise crept higher through the diner's windows, painting Pete's establishment in shades of gold and shadow that transformed the ordinary into something almost beautiful. Somewhere out there in the Virginia mountains, Samuel Carter was driving toward what he thought was salvation, unaware that he was heading into a carefully laid trap with his family's lives hanging in the balance.

Unless Hatch could spring the trap first.

TWELVE

THE ALARM HAD BEEN GOING OFF FOR TWELVE MINUTES when Dr. Samuel Carter finally clawed his way out of a nightmare about tectonic plates and screaming cities.

He jolted upright in the unfamiliar bed, heart hammering against his ribs like a caged bird desperate for escape. The cabin bedroom was gray with pre-dawn light filtering through curtains that smelled of cedar and old summers, and for a disorienting moment he couldn't remember where he was or why his chest felt like it was being crushed by an invisible weight.

Then reality crashed back with the force of a seismic event. The meeting. 7 AM. Ethan Voss and a thumb drive that contained enough evidence to topple governments or start wars, depending on who controlled the narrative.

His eyes landed back on the alarm clock. 6:48 AM. Shit. He'd hit snooze three times without realizing it, lost in dreams that had felt more like prophecies—San Francisco's skyline sliding into the Bay as artificial earthquakes tore the city apart. His own voice echoed through the nightmare, explaining to congressional committees how pressure-relief technology had been perverted into an instrument of mass destruction.

The meeting was in twelve minutes, and he was almost two miles from Pete's Diner.

"Mmm?" Laura stirred beside him, her auburn hair spread across the pillow like spilled wine. Even half-asleep, she was still as beautiful as she had been fifteen years ago.

"Nothing," he whispered, his voice strained from holding his world together with good intentions and rapidly fraying nerves. "Just—I overslept. Wanted to grab breakfast from that diner we passed yesterday."

She cracked one eye open. "Sam. We're on vacation. The whole point is not living by the clock."

"I know, I just thought—coffee. Real coffee, not the instant stuff they stock in these cabins. Before Miles wakes up and discovers there's no Wi-Fi signal strong enough to support his gaming addiction."

That got through to her. Laura's relationship with caffeine was as sacred as his relationship with scientific accuracy, and she understood the value of stealing quiet moments before their eight-year-old son transformed the peaceful mountain morning into a whirlwind of questions, complaints, and demands for entertainment.

"Mmmm. Coffee." She blew him a sleepy kiss that tasted of possibility and normal life. "Cream and two sugars. And maybe one of those cinnamon rolls if they have them fresh."

"Got it."

Carter rolled out of bed and banged his shin on the unfamiliar dresser, a piece of rustic furniture that had probably been handcrafted by someone who believed in the virtue of sharp corners. The curse that escaped his lips was strangled into a whisper.

In the darkness, he grabbed yesterday's jeans from the chair where he'd draped them, along with a Georgetown University sweatshirt that had seen better decades. The fabric was soft with age and washing, a comfort garment that reminded him of simpler times, when his biggest worry had been whether his seismic stress models would get published in the Journal of Geophysical Research.

His bare foot found the corner of their suitcase—another muffled profanity that would have made his mother reach for soap if she'd been alive to hear it. The cabin was a maze of unfamiliar obstacles in the pre-dawn gloom, every surface a potential hazard for someone moving with the careful urgency of a man trying not to wake his family while racing against time.

The thumb drive was in his laptop bag, tucked into an interior pocket he'd modified himself with the obsessive attention to detail that had made him a successful researcher. The files themselves—printouts, emails, technical specifications that could rewrite the geopolitical landscape—stayed hidden in the false bottom he'd constructed using techniques learned from a YouTube video about smuggling contraband across international borders.

Insurance, in case something went wrong. In case the digital transfer failed, or Voss turned out to be something other than the crusading journalist he'd claimed to be.

Carter pocketed the drive along with his keys and phone. He slipped out of the bedroom and through the cabin's main room, where dying embers in the fieldstone fireplace cast dancing shadows on knotty pine walls. The space smelled of woodsmoke and the lingering remnants of last night's s'mores, normal family vacation scents that belonged to a world where fathers didn't carry state secrets and mothers didn't have to worry about their children becoming leverage in corporate wars.

His SUV started with a diesel clatter that seemed too loud in the mountain silence, a mechanical intrusion in a landscape that had existed for millions of years without the benefit of internal combustion engines. He backed out of the gravel driveway, headlights sweeping across trees in the morning mist.

The mountain roads were a different challenge in early morning light than they had been in yesterday's darkness. Low clouds pressed against the peaks like a gray ceiling, and mist clung to the slopes in tendrils that shifted and coiled with each breath of wind. What had seemed merely treacherous in yesterday's sunshine now revealed itself as dangerous—curves that came sharp and sudden, with nothing but air on the passenger side that disappeared into gray vapor, making the drops seem bottomless and infinite.

A yellow diamond warned of deer crossings, its reflective surface beaded with moisture that caught his headlights like tiny stars. Another sign marked a vicious S-curve that had probably claimed its share of overconfident drivers over the decades. The mist thickened as he descended toward the valley, rolling down the mountainside like a slow avalanche of gray cotton that turned familiar landmarks into alien geography.

Carter took it slow, hands tight on the wheel, every muscle in his shoulders clenched with the effort of maintaining control on roads that seemed designed to punish hesitation and overconfidence in equal measure. At one point, a weathered wooden cross stood beside the road, plastic flowers faded by sun and rain serving as testament to someone who hadn't made that turn successfully. The guardrail was absent in that spot, just a few reflector posts marking where asphalt gave way to a drop that vanished into the mist below.

The fog grew denser as he descended, his headlights carving brief tunnels through walls of vapor that seemed solid enough to touch. Somewhere above, the mountain peaks had disappeared entirely, swallowed by clouds that pressed down like the sky was collapsing under its own weight. The world had shrunk to just the reach of his headlights and the yellow lines that guided him through the gray void.

Pete's Diner appeared like a mirage through the lifting mist, its neon sign fighting a losing battle against the growing daylight. The parking lot held a scatter of vehicles—a couple of sedans that probably belonged to traveling salesmen or government workers, a massive truck with its engine idling and exhaust mixing with the fog like mechanical breath. Normal early-morning traffic for a place that served coffee and calories to people who worked while the rest of the world slept.

Nothing that screamed "trap" or "ambush" or any of the other paranoid scenarios that had been playing on a loop in his mind during the drive down from the cabin.

Carter pulled into a parking space and sat for a moment. He could still leave. Drive back to the cabin, wake his family, pack up their vacation gear and run. Find another journalist, another way to expose what AeroSight had turned his life's work into.

But Voss had been so passionate about the story, so committed to exposing the truth about corporate malfeasance and government complicity. The journalist had spent forty-five minutes on the phone describing the moral imperative of bringing hidden crimes into the light, the sacred duty of democracy to hold the powerful accountable for their actions.

Carter killed the engine and stepped out into air that tasted of pine needles and morning dew, with an underlying sharpness that promised frost before the sun reached its zenith.

Chapter 13

Hatch had been nursing the same cup of coffee for twenty minutes, watching the diner's morning rhythm through the mirrored backsplash while her mind catalogued every face, every movement, every detail that might matter when the shooting started. The morning crowd was thin—a few truckers comparing routes over eggs and hash, some early-shift workers grabbing caffeine before facing another day of honest labor. Normal people living normal lives.

She'd positioned herself at the counter with clear sight lines to both exits, back protected by the wall and a clear view of the parking lot through windows that had been cleaned recently enough to provide unobstructed surveillance.

Darlene approached with her order pad ready, coffee pot never far from reach. The fluorescent harshness revealed fine lines that the softer early morning illumination had hidden.

"Can I top you off, or are you ready to order?" Darlene asked. The overnight shift had taken its toll, and it showed in her eyes.

"Yes and yes," Hatch replied.

"Honey, you want the special? Pete's trying to clean out the walk-in before the weekend delivery truck comes." Darlene held her order pad like a shield against the morning's exhaustion. "Yesterday's fries became today's home fries. Waste not, want not, right? Two eggs any style, toast, and enough grease to lubricate a semi-truck for six ninety-nine."

"Sold. Eggs over easy."

"Coming right up." Darlene moved to refill the coffee pot, her movements automatic after years of the same routine.

Hatch finished the last sip and slid her mug over. The coffee streamed black and potent, steam rising like incense from the altar of caffeine worship.

"You're up early for someone who was here past midnight," Darlene observed, noting the details that good waitresses collected like poker tells. "Everything okay?"

"Couldn't sleep. Mountain air, I guess."

"That, or whatever's got you looking over your shoulder every thirty seconds." Darlene's tone was casual, but her eyes held the sharpness of someone who'd learned to read trouble before it announced itself. "You running from something, honey?"

"Running toward something, actually."

"Well, just remember—this is a truck stop, not the OK Corral. Whatever business you got, keep it outside if it's the messy kind."

The door chimed before Hatch could respond, admitting a gust of cool mountain air and the massive silhouette of Rafferty. Gray light of a sunless morning flooded the diner for a moment before being eclipsed by his bulk as he ducked slightly to clear the frame, Princess Mayhem tucked against his chest.

"Morning, Darlene," the giant rumbled in a voice that belonged in a country music ballad.

"Raff! Twice in twelve hours? People will talk."

"Let 'em. Princess Mayhem needed her beauty sleep, and I needed to check on my favorite waitress."

Raff strode to the counter with dog in hand. "I ever tell you the time this little one saved my life?" Raff asked, scratching behind the dog's ears with one finger.

"Tennessee, right?"

"That's the one."

Darlene smiled as she poured his coffee, the expression of

someone who'd heard the story before but never tired of it. "That dog's got better instincts than most people I know."

"Don't I know it. She starts carrying on, I pay attention. Princess knows things before they happen."

Raff settled onto a stool two seats down from Hatch, leaving the polite distance that truckers maintained in the unwritten code of highway courtesy. The stool groaned under his weight but held—industrial furniture built to withstand the kind of punishment that only truck stops and prison cafeterias demanded.

Darlene poured his coffee with the efficiency of a bartender who'd been serving the same customers for decades, then produced a small ceramic dish from under the counter. "Water for Princess Mayhem?"

"If it's not too much trouble."

She filled the dish and set it on the counter. Raff lifted the tiny Chihuahua so she could reach the water, her pink tongue darting in and out like she was afraid someone might steal her drink.

"Don't mind Princess," Raff said to Hatch, noticing her observation. "She's my security detail."

Hatch turned, taking in the full picture—three hundred pounds of trucker holding five pounds of attitude wrapped in rhinestones and fur. "Looks like you've got that situation well under control."

His laugh came softer than she'd expected, almost musical in its warmth. "Princess Mayhem doesn't know she's small. Thinks she's a Rottweiler trapped in a Chihuahua body."

"Smart dog. It's not the size of the dog—"

"It's the size of the fight in the dog." He grinned, the expression transforming his weathered features. "Name's Rafferty. Most folks just call me Raff."

"Hatch. People tend to stick with that."

"Well, Hatch, I saw you in here a few hours back." He raised his voice, making sure it carried to the kitchen where Pete was undoubtedly eavesdropping on his customers' conversations. "Didn't think anyone was brave enough to face Pete's cooking twice in one night."

"I heard that!" Pete's voice boomed from the kitchen, carrying the mock indignation of a man who'd been taking abuse from truckers for longer than most people had been alive. "Keep talking, Raff. See if your eggs don't end up extra crispy."

"You wouldn't dare. I'm your best customer."

"You're my biggest customer. There's a difference."

"Ten pounds of this gut is directly your fault, Pete. Maybe fifteen." Raff patted his substantial midsection with the resignation of a man who'd accepted that truck stop food was both his weakness and his destiny.

"Try thirty!" Pete called back, the sound of sizzling bacon punctuating his words.

"See what I put up with?" Raff said to Hatch, shaking his head in exaggerated despair. "Been coming here for five years. Can't seem to break the habit."

"Could be worse habits to have."

"True enough." He adjusted Princess Mayhem on his lap, the dog having finished her drink and now turning her attention to the morning's entertainment. "You know, this little furball saved my life once. Down in Tennessee, middle of nowhere, truck broke down in a blizzard. Cell phone dead, no help for miles."

His voice carried the weight of genuine gratitude beneath the casual storytelling tone. "Little thing started barking like the world was ending. Wouldn't stop, no matter what I did. Turns out there was a state trooper just over the ridge, maybe two hundred yards away. Her barking led him right to us. Probably would've froze to death otherwise."

"Smart dog," Hatch said, noting how the tiny animal's ears had perked up, as if sensing something in the morning air the humans had missed. Princess Mayhem's attention was focused on the window, her small body tense with alertness.

"Don't I know it. She starts carrying on, I pay attention. Princess knows things before they happen." He scratched behind the dog's ears with surprising gentleness. "Saved my bacon more than once. Got instincts like you wouldn't believe."

"You visiting our little corner of paradise, or just passing through?" he asked Hatch, settling back into the easy conversation that helped pass time in places where time moved slower than the rest of the world.

"Passing through."

"Where to, if you don't mind my asking?"

"Colorado."

His eyebrows rose slightly. "Home?"

"Used to be."

The confusion on his face was almost comical. Hatch clarified. "Army moved me around enough that home became more of a concept than a location."

"Ah." Understanding dawned like sunrise over mountains. "Know that feeling better than most. Long-haul trucking, you learn that roots are a luxury most of us can't afford. Haven't had a permanent address in five years." He sipped his coffee, studying her with new interest. "What's calling you back to Colorado?"

"My niece's birthday."

His expression softened, the way it always did when tough men talked about the children they loved. "Family. Funny how it keeps us tied to places long after we think we've left them behind."

"Something like that."

The door chimed again. In the reflection of the mirrored back-splash, Hatch watched a nervous-looking man enter. Mid-thirties, rumpled clothes that suggested he'd slept poorly, the kind of restless energy that came from too much coffee or not enough sleep. He glanced around the diner like he was looking for someone specific, his movements carrying the particular anxiety of a man walking into danger.

Carter. Had to be. The timing was perfect, and his body language screamed amateur trying to play in a professional game. Too jittery for a casual breakfast, too obvious in his surveillance of the other customers.

Darlene appeared with Hatch's plate—eggs cooked exactly right, home fries crispy enough to use as armor plating, wheat toast cut diagonal. "Here you go, hon. Raff, yours'll be up in just a minute."

She rounded the counter, approaching the newcomer with the

automatic hospitality of someone who'd been serving strangers for decades. Hatch forked a mouthful of home fries while keeping her peripheral attention on the mirror, watching Carter choose a booth in the back corner.

Smart positioning. View of the door, back to the wall, clear sight lines to most of the diner. Except he was too nervous to sell the act. His fingers drummed against the table in a rhythm that suggested barely controlled panic, and he checked his phone every thirty seconds like he was expecting either salvation or damnation to arrive via text message.

THIRTEEN

CARTER SAT IN A BOOTH FACING THE DOOR. INSIDE, warmth and the smell of bacon grease wrapped around him like a familiar blanket. A tired-looking waitress stood behind the counter, pouring coffee for a woman who sat alone at the far end. The woman had a scar on her right arm. She didn't look up as he entered.

"Morning, hon," the waitress called out, her voice carrying the professional cheerfulness of someone who'd been working since before most people went to bed. "Sit anywhere you like. I'll be right with you."

Carter chose a booth in the back corner, where he could see the door and most of the diner's interior. The vinyl was cracked but clean. The table scarred by decades of coffee cups and whispered conversations. He picked up a laminated menu without really seeing it, his attention focused on the entrance and the parking lot beyond the windows.

The door chimed softly as it opened, admitting the cool mountain air and a new customer. Carter's head snapped up, expecting to see Ethan Voss's familiar face.

Instead, an unfamiliar man with a military styled haircut walked straight to Carter's booth and slid in across from him without invitation, moving with the fluid confidence of someone accustomed to taking charge of situations through presence alone.

"Dr. Carter."

It wasn't a question. This man knew exactly who he was looking at.

Before Carter could respond, the waitress appeared beside their table with her order pad and professional smile. "Morning, gentlemen. What can I get started for you?"

The stranger answered smoothly, his voice carrying the cultured accent of someone who'd spent time in expensive schools and exclusive clubs. "Just coffee. To go, if you don't mind."

Darlene's smile faltered slightly—customers who ordered to-go usually didn't sit down first—but she shrugged with practiced indifference. "Two coffees to go, coming right up."

As soon as she left, Carter found his voice, though it came out thinner than he'd intended. "Where's Voss?"

"Didn't you hear?" The man's expression was pleasant, conversational, like they were discussing weather or sports scores instead of life and death. "Tragic fishing accident. Slipped on some rocks, hit his head. Drowned before anyone could help. The Potomac can be treacherous this time of year."

The blood drained from Carter's face as if someone had opened a valve. The words hit him like physical blows, each syllable driving home the reality that his careful plan had just collapsed into a nightmare. He started to stand, every instinct screaming at him to run, to get away from this man and this place before whatever trap was closing could snap shut around him.

"Don't." The word was quiet but carried the weight of absolute authority, the tone of someone accustomed to being obeyed without question. "Don't do something stupid that we'll both regret. This can be easy, or it can be very, very difficult. The choice is entirely yours."

The man's hands stayed visible on the table, but Carter noticed how they rested—ready to move, ready to reach for whatever was concealed beneath that expensive jacket. The positioning was casual but purposeful, like a gunslinger in an old Western who didn't need to touch his weapon to communicate the threat.

"Lovely family you have," the man continued, his voice never losing its conversational tone. "Your wife, Laura. Your boy—Miles, isn't it? Eight years old. Asthma. Such a fragile condition in a child that age. Be a shame if something tragic happened at that isolated cabin where they're sleeping so peacefully right now."

Carter's voice cracked with the force of emotions too large for his throat to contain. "If you hurt them—"

"You'll what?" The man leaned forward, his eyes holding the flat interest of a scientist observing a specimen under a microscope. "Let me be clear, Doctor. The people I work for aren't in the threat business. We're in the elimination business. Give us what you brought, and we disappear like a bad dream. Your family enjoys their vacation, everyone goes home happy. Refuse, and the pain they feel will be entirely proportional to your level of cooperation."

Carter's hands shook as the magnitude of his situation became clear. The thumb drive felt like it weighed a thousand pounds, its plastic case suddenly hot against his leg through the fabric of his jacket pocket.

"But this isn't the place for that conversation," the man said, glancing around the diner with the casual assessment of someone who understood the value of avoiding witnesses. "Too many eyes, too many potential complications. We'll conclude our business outside, somewhere more private."

Darlene returned with two paper cups, steam rising from the small openings in their plastic lids. "Here you go, gentlemen. Anything else I can get you?"

"We're all set." The man left a twenty on the table—far more than the coffee cost, the kind of tip that ensured good service and discouraged questions. He stood smoothly, his right hand drifting to his pocket in a casual gesture that wasn't casual at all. "After you, Doctor. And do carry the coffee. Wouldn't want to waste Darlene's excellent work."

Carter stood on legs that felt like water, picking up both cups with hands that trembled enough to slosh coffee against the lids. The liquid was hot enough to burn, but he barely felt it against his fingers.

"Remember what's at stake," the man whispered, close enough that Carter could smell his aftershave—something expensive and European that probably cost more than most people spent on groceries. "Your cooperation determines whether this stays civilized or becomes something that requires an explanation to paramedics."

They walked toward the exit, Carter moving without conscious direction, his feet carrying him toward whatever waited outside. In the mirrored wall behind the counter, he caught the woman with the scar shifting on her stool. But what could she do? What could anyone do when men with guns decided that your life was worth less than their payday?

The door chimed their departure like a funeral bell. Morning sun hit Carter's face, momentarily blinding him after the diner's warm interior. Outside, the mist was beginning to lift, but heavy clouds still clung to the mountain peaks above them like a promise of storms to come. The parking lot stretched before them, empty of help, empty of hope.

Just Carter, a trained killer, and a thumb drive full of secrets that men would murder to protect.

HATCH HAD WATCHED the new arrival slide into Carter's booth without invitation through the mirrored glass. After a brief verbal exchange, she could see Carter's whole body go rigid, likely his fight-or-flight response kicking in with nowhere to run and no realistic option to fight.

"More coffee?" Darlene asked, appearing at Hatch's elbow with the pot that seemed permanently welded to her hand.

"Thanks."

She poured the refill while Hatch divided her attention between the casual conversation with Raff and whatever was unfolding in the back booth. Darlene headed to the newcomers, and Hatch caught fragments of conversation—something about coffee to go. Odd request for someone who'd just sat down, but it made sense if you were planning to take your conversation somewhere more private.

"Your trucker special, Raff." Pete emerged from the kitchen with a plate that could have fed a small family. "Try not to die of cholesterol before you pay your tab."

"You're all heart, Pete."

Hatch ate mechanically, her body going through the motions of normalcy while her mind calculated angles and options. The operative was talking, his posture relaxed but ready, while Carter seemed to shrink beneath each word. When Darlene returned with two to-go cups, Carter's hands shook as he reached for them.

Hatch watched from her seat as Carter stood. The man who'd joined him had his hand drifting toward his right pocket. Carter looked like a man walking to his execution, every line of his body screaming reluctance and terror.

They headed for the door—Carter first, the other man close behind, guiding without touching in the classic formation of professional escort work. No obvious coercion, nothing that would alarm casual observers, just two men leaving a diner together.

Hatch waited exactly three seconds after the door closed, giving them time to clear the immediate area. She slid cash under her mug and stood.

"Whoa, you just got here," Raff said, surprised by her sudden departure. "Hope it wasn't something I said. Or the company?"

"Absolutely not." She stood, adjusting her jacket to ensure her weapon stayed concealed while remaining accessible. "Something came up. Work stuff."

"Well, damn. Was nice talking to someone who understands the life." His disappointment seemed genuine—the reaction of a lonely man who'd found a kindred spirit only to watch her disappear again.

"Likewise. Maybe we'll cross paths again."

"I'm here every few weeks. You know where to find me."

She headed for the door, the walk of someone who had somewhere important to be but wasn't in a panic to get there. Through the window, she could see Carter and the operative in the parking lot.

Time to go to work.

The door chimed her exit, the sound mixing with the cool mountain air that knifed through the opening, carrying the scent of pine needles and approaching weather. Behind her, normal life continued its eternal rhythm—Raff attacking his breakfast with the dedication of a man who viewed calories as fuel for the road ahead, Pete banging pans in the kitchen with the percussion of honest labor, Darlene pouring endless coffee for people who needed caffeine more than they needed sleep.

But outside, in the crisp mountain morning where frost still clung to the shadows, a different story was unfolding. One that would likely end in blood unless she changed the script from execution to rescue.

Hatch moved into the parking lot

Princess Mayhem's barking suddenly pierced the morning air, sharp and insistent, carrying across the parking lot like an air raid siren. Through the diner window, Hatch could see the tiny dog pressed against the glass, every line of her small body radiating alarm.

Raff had been right. Princess Mayhem knew things before they happened.

And right now, she was trying to warn everyone that something very bad was about to unfold in the shadow of the Virginia mountains.

FOURTEEN

Cold air knifed under Hatch's jacket as she eased around to the back of the lot. The sky was bruising toward daylight, but dark clouds and morning fog pushed back against the weak orange lifting behind the tree line. The lot breathed steam. Rigs idled. Frost clung to windshields like sugar.

Thirty yards out, Samuel Carter was being walked toward a dark sedan. The man at his elbow kept the touch light, friendly on the surface. It read wrong from here. Tinted windows. Engine running. The driver's head had that slight tilt of a man using mirrors for more than traffic.

Hatch slid off the curb, boots quiet on grit. She didn't sprint. Didn't shout. She just adjusted her path as if headed to her Jeep, then drifted into their lane, each step shaving the distance.

Carter's SUV sat two rows over, nose-out. He cut her a glance—quick, panicked, pretending not to see her. The elbow man squeezed once, guiding him on. They were ten yards from the sedan. Then eight.

She clocked the sedan as she moved. It was unoccupied. Rear door ajar.

Hatch's skin went cold before the metal touched it.

"Hands where I can see 'em," a voice said behind her, easy as a bartender. The pressure of a pistol muzzle kissed the base of her skull, low and centered. Close enough, she could feel the texture of the front sight.

Hatch stopped. Breath in. Hands eased out, palms open and empty at shoulder height. The elbow man half turned, reading her posture and the new geometry at once.

The voice behind her stayed conversational. "Don't be cute. I like my mornings quiet."

Dishware clinked inside the diner, Rafferty's truck chuffed, a bird tried out a single note and thought better of it. Hatch took it all in as her sensory input kicked into overdrive. The muted shadow of the man holding the gun to her head

"Let's make this easy," the voice behind her murmured. "Hands stay up. We all go for a drive. No noise."

Carter looked at Hatch. His foot turned out. His body was preparing to run.

"Well, this worked out smashingly. We've got both targets and coffee to go," the man guiding Carter by the elbow said. "Time to go."

The muzzle of the pistol nudged Hatch forward. She reluctantly gave in.

Carter took one step in the direction of the sedan before throwing the coffee cups in the direction of his captor.

Scalding streams leapt sideways, the liquid hit the man's face and neck with a wet slap. He screamed and reeled backward, both hands up. The second cup bounced off his chest. The lid popped. A brown fan exploded across his shirt.

Hatch made a move to capitalize on the distraction, but the gunman didn't take the bait. The muzzle never left the back of her head. "Don't give me a reason to paint this lot your shade of red."

Carter ran.

He popped his SUV with the key fob as he sprinted, flung the driver's door wide, slid behind the wheel, and jammed the starter. Tires barked. Frost pitched off the hood in a glittering sheet. The engine howled.

The coffee-drenched man staggered two steps, pivoted, and swore before scrabbling for the sedan.

"Get in," the rear voice said. "Backseat. Now."

Hatch knew opportunity when it was presented. And right now, she had none. Compliance was her only option. She hoped time would gift her with another chance. She followed the instructions of the gunman at her back and entered the vehicle, deliberately keeping her movements slow if for no other reason than to buy Carter some additional seconds.

The sedan's backseat was black vinyl gone glossy with age. Hatch ducked in sideways, scooted across, and felt the muzzle slide from her skull to the ribs beneath her arm, finding a new resting place. The gunman joined her in the back while the coffee man drove.

Carter's SUV fishtailed out of the lot. The sedan gave chase. In the diner window, the patrons inside continued their morning unaware of what just transpired in the lot outside.

Coffee steamed off the driver's collar. A red patch bloomed on the side of his neck. He smelled like burned sugar and expensive aftershave. "That bitch moves, you put a bullet in her."

The pistol reestablished itself against Hatch's ribs, the pressure measured, not angry. "Do me a favor and keep your hands on your knees," he said. "You don't move, you don't die. At least for now."

Hatch set them there. Palms down. Sleeves riding halfway up her forearms exposing the scar on her right. He looked at it and seemed to be admiring it.

The driver took the exit slowly, peering both ways, playing the part of an ordinary man leaving an ordinary breakfast. Then he rolled onto the highway and put his foot down.

Carter's SUV vanished into a dip in the road, only to pop back into view a quarter mile up. He was pushing speed and panic in equal measure.

The driver pulled his cellphone out and placed a call. "He slipped us at the diner. Heading your way." There was a pause while the man on the other end spoke. "She's with us." He listened. "Copy. We're keeping a loose follow. He's leading us right to the cabin. We'll deal with it then."

Hatch kept her breath even. Every second her captors didn't hit panic tempo was a second she could use later.

A mile of road hissed under them. Then two. The sky got brighter without warming anything. Frost retreated into the ditch grass. They passed the deer sign, reflective and harmless in the day. She mapped the turns without moving her head—left at the split with the leaning mailbox, right where the pavement was patched and rough. A roadside cross flashed past, plastic flowers stiff in the cold. She put all of it in the same place you put oxygen and exits.

"Comfy?" the elbow man asked. His voice had come back to casual. He liked the undercard. He liked being the part of the machine that turned.

"Seat's a little stiff," Hatch said.

He smiled with his mouth and not his eyes. "Noted."

They held speed for three more curves. On the fourth, the lane narrowed, and the shoulder fell away into timber.

Hatch breathed. She let her shoulders sag a fraction. Staying ready meant staying loose.

FIFTEEN

THE SEDAN ATE THE ROAD IN SMOOTH, STEADY SWALLOWS. Inside, the air tasted of old vinyl and gun oil. Hatch sat back-right, hands loose on her knees, the way you sit when you want a man with a pistol to think you've stopped trying.

Up front, the driver kept Carter's vehicle in sight. Not crowding. Not losing him. Steering wheel relaxed in his hands as if he'd been born with it.

"You've got another team with the family," Hatch said. "Is that what we do now in honor of national security? We kill women and children?"

"Shut up," the driver told the windshield.

"That what it says on your business card? Patriot for hire?" Hatch asked. "Doesn't matter who bleeds so long as the check clears and the flag's somewhere on the brochure?"

Backseat Guy's jaw worked. "You don't know a thing about it."

"I know what it looks like from the ground," she said. "I know the sound a child makes when the oxygen stops. I know how fast your story turns on you when people stop believing the word 'necessary.'" Hatch tilted her head just enough to force him to adjust the muzzle. "I know lies don't block bullets."

The driver's eyes flicked to the mirror. "I said shut up."

"You hide behind orders," Hatch said softly. "Cute shield. You think it makes you smaller targets? It doesn't. It just makes you easier to aim at."

Backseat Guy lifted his free hand—palm flat, the start of a backhand he'd probably been saving since she opened her mouth.

There. The gun hand drifted a fraction, angled off center. The weight came off his knee.

Hatch's right heel snapped inside his leg, driving his knee sideways toward the door. Cartilage complained. His breath left him in a single animal sound. The gun dipped. She threw an elbow into the soft place under his ribs—short, mean, all hip. The pistol jumped. She clamped her left hand on his wrist and dragged the muzzle off target.

Up front, the driver twisted, eyes off the road. "Hey!"

The sedan hit loose gravel at the apex of a blind curve. The wheel stuttered. Tires screeched. The shoulder was a suggestion. The drop on the far side wasn't.

Backseat Guy grabbed at her throat with his free hand. She shoved the gun toward the floorboard and drove her forehead into the bridge of his nose. His grip faltered.

The sedan swerved as the driver reached for her. Hatch snapped head up just in time to see the curve of the road.

The driver threw his head back around just in time to see nothing but sky and treetops where road should be. He overcorrected. The right tires kissed air. Weight shifted. Momentum decided it liked the downhill.

Hatch shouldered the door. It bounced once on the latch.

Backseat Guy lunged, but his knee didn't know the plan. She hit the latch again, harder. The seal broke with a sucking sound. Cold morning tore into the car.

The sedan slid—not a neat skid but a long, inevitable slide with the front end already light. The driver stomped on the brake—too late, wrong choice—turning speed into noise.

Hatch pushed off the seat with both feet and let gravity win.

She fell hard into dew-covered grass, rolled twice, and came up skidding on her side, boots carving lines in burnished frost. The world tilted. The edge rushed at her like an open mouth. She threw both hands out. Fingers found a thick root jutting from the cut bank and locked.

Her body kept moving. Her shoulders nearly pulled out of their sockets. Pain lit every nerve from elbow to spine. Dirt and pebbles avalanched past her, pattering into silence.

The sedan went over. Tires left earth with a howl like something alive. Metal screamed as it bounced once, twice, then vanished into timber with the hollow thud of big things meeting bigger things. The smell of hot brakes rolled back up the slope with a puff of oil and radiator steam.

THE MOUNTAIN ROAD stretched ahead like a gray ribbon bleeding into the Virginia wilderness, empty of traffic except for the occasional hawk circling overhead and the distant contrails of aircraft following invisible highways thirty thousand feet above. Carter kept checking the rearview mirror, waiting for the black sedan to reappear around one of the countless curves that wound between hills older than human memory.

Through the fog, the headlights of his pursuers rounded a bend. They'd gained on him. Just as they came into view, the vehicle skidded sideways across wet asphalt, the whole frame tilting like a ship caught broadside by a rogue wave, before vanishing over the lip of the cliff as if the earth had simply opened its mouth and swallowed them whole.

He slowed to a stop. He'd heard the scream of metal shearing against stone, the explosive shatter of safety glass designed to protect passengers from everything except gravity, then the hollow boom from far below.

Then nothing. The sound had rolled away into the canyon like distant thunder, leaving only the empty hiss of wind through pine branches.

Carter should have felt relief. One less threat between him and his family. One fewer vector of violence aimed at the people he loved most in the world.

Instead, guilt hooked into him and twisted hard, boring through his chest like a surgical drill designed to reach the conscience. The woman who'd been in that sedan—tall, lean, with eyes that stayed steady even under the kind of pressure that turned most people into panicked animals—had risked herself to buy him a few precious seconds of freedom. She'd thrown herself into harm's way for a man she'd never met, a stranger whose only qualification for rescue was that he was being hunted by the same people who'd apparently marked her for death.

She hadn't deserved to die for him. Hell, she probably hadn't deserved to die at all.

Carter gripped the steering wheel tighter, knuckles going white with the effort of maintaining control over both the vehicle and his spiraling emotions. If by some miracle she'd survived the crash—and survival seemed about as likely as spontaneous human flight—she was clearly resourceful enough to find her own way out of whatever hole physics had dropped her into. But that was hope, not a plan, the kind of desperate optimism that kept people functional when reality became too sharp to bear.

Right now, the only plan that mattered was getting to Laura and Miles before anyone else did.

SIXTEEN

HATCH HUNG THERE, LUNGS WORKING IN SHORT, STUPID bursts. The root creaked the way old wood does when asked to do new jobs. The ground under her boots gave another inch, then thought better of it.

Hatch's right hand slipped a knuckle's worth. She clenched harder. Splinters bit skin. Blood slicked bark. The slope angled away under her toes, a bad invitation.

She swung her left heel into the dirt and found nothing. Tried again—heel, toe, heel—until a clump of roots caught rubber and held. Her forearms burned. She risked a breath that wasn't all noise.

From below came no voices. No groans. Just the long sigh of a car cooling in places it shouldn't.

A pebble clicked past her cheek and dropped into the quiet.

She looked up. The lip of the road sat two feet above her fingers. Two feet might as well have been two flights if the root gave.

Hatch let her head fall against her wrist for one second and let the second be exactly that: a second. Then she pulled.

Slow, not pretty, not clean. Right hand up a quarter inch. Left hand up a quarter inch to meet it. Boot heel walked higher in the soft collapse. Elbows locked, back did the idiot work a back does when the rest of you would rather quit.

The root groaned a warning she ignored. She slid her forearms onto the ledge and levered, shoulders screaming. Her chest hit gravel. For one sweet half-breath she was a plank. Then her hips, then one knee. She hooked that knee over the lip like a drowning thing catching a ladder rung and rolled onto her side, the world going from vertical to horizontal in a messy stitch.

She lay there, face to the cold grit, and laughed once without humor. Then she pushed to her knees and crawled the last two feet into the shoulder grass, away from the edge, away from the root that had decided to keep its job for one more morning.

The mountain air cut clean through her. She sucked it in anyway.

Far below, maybe three hundred feet down the slope, she could see the sedan's final resting place. The vehicle had rolled multiple times during its descent, carving a scar through the timber before coming to rest upside down against a cluster of pines. One wheel still spun lazily, catching morning light with each revolution. Steam rose from the wreckage in thin white ghosts.

No movement. No voices calling for help. Nothing but the twisted metal parts scattered across the forest floor.

Hatch rolled to a sit and looked back over the edge. Broken branches marked the sedan's path like breadcrumbs leading to a particularly violent fairy tale ending. The smell of hot oil and antifreeze drifted up on the morning air, mixing with pine sap and the mineral scent of disturbed earth.

She pushed to her feet, legs shaky but functional. Her right shoulder felt like someone had tried to remove it with a crowbar, and her palms were raw from gripping the root. Blood had dried in dark crescents under her fingernails.

But she was breathing. Walking. Thinking clearly enough to process what had just happened and what came next.

Down the road, a gray ribbon of settling dust marked Carter's path. He was still running, still heading straight toward whatever trap Kern had prepared.

She dusted herself off, brushing gravel and pine needles from her jacket, wiping blood from her scraped palms on her jeans. Her shoulder protested every movement, but everything still worked. Everything still functioned.

The road stretched ahead, empty and winding through the Virginia hills. Carter's dust trail ended at the pavement, but tire tracks in the gravel shoulder told the story of his passage.

Which, in his case, it probably was.

Hatch broke into a steady jog, boots finding their rhythm on the asphalt. The mountain air burned cold in her lungs, but the movement felt good after the cramped confines of the sedan. Her body remembered this—the long pursuit, the patient hunt, the steady expenditure of energy in service of a larger goal.

The road climbed through stands of pine and oak, past weathered signs warning of deer crossings and steep grades. Her breath misted in the morning air as she settled into the pace that had carried her across Afghan mountainsides and through urban battlefields where endurance mattered more than speed.

A half mile ahead, through a gap in the trees, she caught a glimpse of taillights disappearing around a curve. Too far to identify but moving fast enough to be Carter fleeing toward what he thought was salvation.

She pushed harder, ignoring the protest from her battered shoulder.

Around the next bend, a brown Forest Service sign appeared through the trees, its reflective letters catching what sunlight managed to filter through the canopy:

PINE RIDGE FAMILY CAMPGROUND ELEVATION 2,847 FEET

SITES 1-47 2 MILES AHEAD

Carter wasn't running randomly. He had a destination.

Hatch picked up her pace. Time to find out what was waiting at the end of the road.

. . .

SEVENTEEN

CARTER PRESSED THE ACCELERATOR, FEELING THE SUV respond with the eager surge of an engine that had been built for exactly this kind of driving—mountain roads, emergency situations, the kind of desperate flight that required reliable power and unshakeable traction. The road pitched and snaked through stands of pine and oak that had been growing here when the Constitution had still been fresh ink on parchment, finally spilling into the network of gravel tracks that connected the scattered cabins to something resembling civilization.

The rental complex was exactly what he'd requested when making the reservation—isolated, private, silent. The cabins were spaced far apart, each tucked deep between stands of pine and birch that provided natural privacy screens. No central lodge, no caretaker's shack, no communal firepit where guests might gather and form any bond that led to shared contact information and future communication.

Just gravel loops and a few small driveways cut into the trees, each leading to a structure designed to house temporary refugees from the modern world.

Now, that same isolation felt like a trap.

If something went wrong, no one would see it happening. No one would hear the screams. No one would notice the absence until it was far too late to matter.

Carter swung into the final curve, tires spitting gravel that rattled against the SUV's undercarriage like hail on a tin roof. His cabin appeared between the trees, a modest structure of logs and fieldstone that looked like it had grown from the forest floor rather than being imposed upon it. The chimney cut a gray line against the pale sky.

Everything looked normal. Peaceful. Exactly as he'd left it two hours ago when he'd driven away to meet a dead journalist and walk into a trap that had nearly cost him everything.

He braked hard, throwing the transmission into park before the SUV had fully stopped rocking on its suspension. The sudden deceleration sent his laptop bag sliding across the passenger seat, and for a wild moment he thought about the files it contained—backup copies of everything he'd wanted to give Voss. Evidence that could still bring down David Kern and AeroSight, if it fell into the right hands.

But first, his family.

Carter flung the door open and hit the ground running. The mountain air was sharp in his lungs, carrying the scent of pine needles and wood smoke and a cleanliness that came from being far from cities and their accumulated sins.

"Laura!" His voice split the morning stillness like an axe through kindling. "Miles!"

He charged toward the porch, heart hammering against his ribs with the irregular rhythm of panic barely held in check. " We need to leave right now! Something's happened, I'll explain on the way—just get your stuff!"

No answer. Not even the sound of movement inside the cabin.

The silence felt wrong, pregnant with menace that made his skin crawl. Laura should have heard him coming up the gravel drive. Miles should have been awake by now, probably complaining about the lack of Wi-Fi or demanding to know why they had to leave their vacation early.

He hit the first step of the porch, then froze as his peripheral vision caught something that didn't belong.

Out of the corner of his eye, barely visible beyond the cabin's rear corner, was the squared-off nose of another vehicle. Black paint, mud sprayed high up the wheel wells like it had been driven hard through terrain that wasn't meant for civilian transportation. No rental company stickers. No license plate visible from this angle. No legitimate reason it should have been here, hidden just out of sight from anyone approaching the cabin's front entrance.

The sight landed in his gut like a stone dropping into still water, sending ripples of dread through his entire nervous system.

THE TRAIL ROSE FAST. Roots braided like snakes. Wet patches slicked with last night's frost melt. The air thinned and went clean, pine sap and cold stone. Branch tips slapped Hatch's sleeves. Her breath settled into a metronome—four beats in, four out—every exhale a knife edge across her ribs.

She counted paces, counted trees. At the first split she went right —the ground there was more chewed, the fern heads broken where something heavier than deer had passed.

A crow barked somewhere to her left, the same five-note laugh it had been doing for five million years. She let it talk.

The path kinked around a toppled trunk and opened into a small flat where the undergrowth had been mashed down into a rough rectangle. A camo tarp lay half off something low and mechanical. She flipped the rest of the tarp with her boot.

ATV. Two-seater. Plastic body scuffed and spidered from smarter days. No plates. Key in the ignition, like a promise. A folded map, sun-faded and torn, sat under a bungee on the front rack, a crude loop drawn in red marker around a section of the ridge. Good men kept maps. Bad men did, too.

She checked the gas—just over a quarter tank left. She put her thumb on the starter.

The engine coughed smoke, then caught with a chainsaw snarl. Not subtle. She swung a leg over, settled low, and rolled the thumb throttle. The machine lurched forward, then smoothed as the belt grabbed. She kept it just shy of screaming—fast enough to matter, quiet enough not to announce open season.

The trail became a series of bad decisions—rocks chucked up at odd angles, dips that wanted to twist the axle out of her hands, brush that reached to strip her from the seat. She leaned where the machine wanted her to, let the suspension take the worst of it, stood over the ruts when the ground went to teeth. Every bump sent a dull hammer through her ribs and shoulder. She took it. The trail guided around the cabins, cutting the distance between her and Carter.

Above the tree line, she caught a glimpse of the paved road cutting the slope like a gray ribbon. Far off, a flicker—a moving speck reflecting sun. Carter's SUV. She was now only a minute or so behind. Long enough to make her timing a question instead of an answer.

The gap between the trees broke without warning. The land fell away to a shallow bowl, and in the bowl a track ran clean as if someone had taken a ruler to the dirt.

She killed the engine before the last rise and let the sudden quiet ring in her ears. Hatch moved off the ATV and got on her belly, she crawled the last dozen yards to a notch between two granite boulders, letting nature provide concealment as she lay quiet and watched.

The cabin's stone chimney peeked up from its dark roof. A posted road looped around a broad clearing. Carter's SUV sat cocked at an angle in the dirt, driver's door open, engine still shivering.

EIGHTEEN

CARTER'S PULSE SPIKED, ADRENALINE FLOODING HIS bloodstream with the bitter taste of fight-or-flight chemistry. He shifted his stance, weight moving to the balls of his feet, eyes tracking between the front door and that blind corner where the mysterious vehicle waited.

Somewhere inside the cabin, the air felt ... occupied. Not with movement, exactly, but with the subtle pressure that came from human presence. The kind of atmospheric disturbance that every parent learned to recognize—the difference between a house that was truly empty and one that contained sleeping children, or in this case, the difference between solitude and surveillance.

The cabin door swung open. A man stood in the shadowed recess just beyond the threshold, his form backlit by the warm glow of the interior lights that Laura must have turned on when she'd woken. Late thirties, lean frame wrapped in a weatherproof jacket that suggested outdoor work or military training. The man's eyes moved constantly, scanning, while his head remained perfectly still.

When he spoke, his voice came out calm, almost conversational, like they were old friends meeting for coffee.

"Come on in, Carter. We've got some things we need to discuss."

Carter's muscles locked, every fiber in his body screaming warnings that bypassed conscious thought. "Where's my wife? My son?"

"They're fine ... for now." The man stepped forward just enough for Carter to see the matte black pistol in his right hand, held low but ready, the casual grip of someone who'd pointed weapons at human beings so many times that it had become as natural as breathing. "But every second you stand there making noise, my partner's trigger finger gets a little itchier."

The words hit Carter like physical blows, each syllable driving home the reality that his worst fears had materialized while he'd been gone. Laura. Miles. His mind shoved their faces into the forefront of his consciousness—Laura's sleepy smile as he'd kissed her goodbye, Miles curled up with his stuffed triceratops, breathing the slightly labored rhythm that always preceded his morning nebulizer treatment.

The thought of them being cornered, threatened, used as leverage against him knotted his stomach until he could barely breathe. They were innocent. They didn't even know what he'd discovered, what he'd tried to do, what forces he'd set in motion by attempting to expose the truth about Project Rift.

"How do I know I can trust you?" he asked, fighting to keep his voice level and reasonable, the tone of a man trying to negotiate rather than someone whose world was collapsing in real time.

The man's smile held no warmth, just the mechanical expression of someone who'd learned to mimic human emotion. He raised two fingers in a mock salute, the gesture carrying enough mockery to fill a stadium.

"Scout's honor."

Moments before, from somewhere deep in the trees behind the cabin, he could have sworn he heard an engine murmur—low, distant, barely audible over the whisper of wind through pine branches. The sound had dissipated. He kept his eyes locked on the man in the doorway, reading body language and micro-expressions the way he read seismic data—looking for patterns, stress points, indicators of what might happen next. Every instinct he possessed screamed at him to bolt for the SUV. Maybe it would be enough to draw these people away from the cabin where his family was being held hostage.

But the thought was a fleeting one. Something told him that anything less than compliance would end terribly. For both him and his family.

The man stepped back just enough to clear the entrance, the movement precise and economical. "That's it. Easy does it. No sudden moves. Just walk through that door like a civilized human being."

Carter forced himself forward, each step feeling heavier than the last, as if gravity itself increased with every inch of progress toward the threshold. Crossing that porch felt like walking into a snare he could see but couldn't avoid—the kind of trap that closed around you regardless of how carefully you moved or how desperately you wanted to escape.

The wooden planks creaked under his boots, a sound that seemed amplified in the mountain stillness. Behind him, his SUV sat with its door open, keys still in the ignition, engine still idling. Evidence of his panicked arrival, of the desperate hope that he could somehow outrun the consequences of his decision to become a whistleblower.

But some consequences, he was learning, had longer legs than fear.

HATCH ARRIVED JUST in time to see Carter step out of his vehicle. From her vantage point behind a large boulder, she looked on as the geologist himself walked slowly from the SUV to the base of the porch steps. He lifted his hands shoulder-high, palms out, and took the first stair with that careful gait of a man who wanted to believe a compromise existed.

The door opened a few inches more. In the dark recesses beyond, Hatch made out a single figure. In the dim light, she saw the pistol in his hand.

They had his family. Now they had Carter.

Hatch backed up, heart steady now that the shape of the problem had a face. Panic was for people who didn't bring tools. Fear was for after.

She slipped downslope along the granite shoulder, keeping the bulk between her and the cabin. The trees opened to a narrow seam of earth where rain had cut a vein. Hatch followed it, soft-footed, letting gravity help until the last thirty feet where she slowed to a prowl.

A trail cam blinked red on a pine trunk near the clearing's edge. She circled it wide. Farther right, a stack of split wood, roofed with a sheet of tin, stank of fresh sap. Good cover. Closer to the back door, the ground sloped to a gravel drive that ran to a shed. A generator hummed inside that shed, a low burr under the cold.

Hatch froze, counted, listened. The door to the cabin closed. She could hear only the muffled rumblings of the conversation taking place within.

Hatch slid behind the wood pile and set her back to the rough timber, angling the Glock in a low ready. She closed her eyes and let the mental map redraw—porch angle, interior door swing, the position of the furniture. She had one shot at entering unseen and buying enough surprise to change the math. After that, it would be noise and movement and the decisions of men who wanted control and might settle for killing to get it back.

She breathed. Once. Twice. Let her shoulders drop the useless tension and keep what she needed.

The generator hiccupped. It wasn't a failure, just the weird little cough small engines do when asked to carry a sudden load. Through a slit in the window curtain, she saw the armed man lean forward to say something, the angle of his hand telling her where his gun pointed.

To her right, a gap in the shrubs showed the back corner of the cabin, a window with a curtain half-drawn. Between the two, the ground ran hard and dark, trackless and good.

They were ready for his arrival. But not mine.

She ghosted along the back wall, counting her steps without a sound. At the corner she stopped and listened again. Footfalls inside—in place, not moving, a guard settling weight from one leg to the other. Closer to the front of the cabin than the rear. Good.

She eased her way to the back door and pressed her fingertips to the knob. Cold metal. No one's used it in the last minute. It didn't seem as though this crew was expecting any unwelcome visitors.

She backed off an inch. The hinge pins on the exterior were rusty but intact. She indexed the lock with her shoulder and listened.

On the front side of the house, a floorboard spoke. Carter's voice reached her as a hush, a pleading shape too soft to carry words. A woman's voice whimpered. Then the boy coughed again. The sound hit Hatch like a hand on the back, pushing her forward.

She slid the knife from her pocket, slipped the thin steel between jamb and strike, and pressed. The latch thought about it, then gave a quarter inch. She pressed again. Metal whispered. The door clicked.

Hatch left it closed. She wasn't going in. Not yet. Not loud.

She moved to the curtain gap, set one eye at the crease, and let the room resolve.

Kitchen table with too many papers. A nebulizer case open, tubing looped like a lazy snake. Carter's wife sat straight-backed on a couch, hands folded. A zip tie restrained her wrists. A young boy, presumably Carter's son., was forced into a standing position alongside her. The boy's mouth parted, breathing effort written in the tight muscles at his throat. A man had a pistol pointed at the back of the child's head.

The man who she'd seen through the door was ushering Carter into the space.

Hatch drew back from the curtain and set her shoulder to the wall.

You didn't open a door in the middle of a sentence. You didn't cut a wire while a spark was on it. You waited for the overlap, for the sound that covered motion, for the breath that made men blink. Then you went in.

Hatch settled into the shadow of the eave and waited for her moment.

But as she listened to the voices inside, Hatch realized waiting for the perfect moment might mean waiting too long. The interrogation was escalating. Every second increased the chance that patience would become complicity in whatever these men planned to do to the Carter family.

She needed a distraction. Something loud and immediate that would pull both operatives' attention away from their prisoners and toward the front of the cabin.

Her eyes settled on Carter's SUV, still idling thirty yards away in the clearing. Driver's door hanging open. Engine running. Pointed almost directly at the cabin's front porch like an arrow cocked and ready to fly.

NINETEEN

THE CABIN CARTER HAD LEFT IN HASTE EARLIER THIS morning was now a tableau of controlled violence, domestic comfort perverted into a hostage situation that had been orchestrated with military precision. The main room stretched twenty feet from the stone fireplace to the kitchen area, with the leather couch positioned against the far wall where it commanded a view of the front windows. He looked in horror at his wife and son.

Another man stood behind Miles with a gun pointed at the back of his head while Laura was bound at the wrists. Tears streamed down both their faces.

The gunman behind his son was tall with lean muscle pushing out from beneath a black tactical sweater, hair buzzed to a gray shadow that suggested military training and disciplined maintenance.

Carter was nudged further into the room by the man who'd greeted him at the front door. The sidearm he'd held was now holstered but visible beneath his jacket, the grip positioned for a fast draw—close enough to access instantly, concealed enough to avoid appearing overtly threatening until the moment called for escalation. He deemed him the leader of whatever this was.

Carter stood frozen just inside the front door, still processing the nightmare his family vacation had become.

Miles' small shoulders hunched forward, his breath coming in the ragged, shallow gasps that sent an instant alarm through Carter's nervous system. Not the full panic of an asthma attack—not yet—but close enough to twist his gut into knots and flood his bloodstream with the helpless terror that came from watching his child struggle for something as basic as oxygen.

The boy's lips held the faint blue tinge that meant his airways were starting to constrict, and each exhale carried the telltale whistle that preceded the kind of crisis that sent them racing to emergency rooms in the middle of the night. His stuffed triceratops lay on the floor beside the couch, knocked there during whatever struggle had preceded the current standoff.

Carter tried to keep his voice calm, reasonable, the tone he used when negotiating with insurance companies or explaining complex geological concepts to congressional committee members who had the attention span of caffeinated squirrels. "Let me give him his nebulizer. It'll settle his breathing. He's not a threat to anyone."

The leader smiled like he'd just been handed the opening move of a chess game he'd already won. His position near the kitchen island allowed him to watch Carter while keeping the couch—and his primary leverage—in his peripheral vision.

"That's not how these things work, Doctor." His voice carried the cultured accent of an expensive education corrupted by professional violence. "You don't get to ask for favors when you've given me nothing in return. This is a negotiation, and right now, you're operating from a position of considerable weakness."

Laura's eyes flashed with the fury of a mother watching her child suffer, fear transforming into something more dangerous. "I don't know what this is about, but you have the wrong people. We're just here on vacation. We haven't done anything to anyone."

The man took two measured steps closer to the couch, closing the distance to six feet—close enough to demonstrate his control, far enough to maintain tactical spacing. He cocked his head at Laura with patronizing interest, then shifted his attention back to Carter.

"Keeping secrets from your wife, Doctor? Not a particularly telling sign of a stable marriage. I wonder what other important details you've neglected to share with the woman who shares your bed."

Laura turned toward Carter, confusion breaking through her fear like sunlight through storm clouds. "Sam? What is he talking about? What secrets?"

Carter's shoulders slumped under the weight of months of deception; all the careful lies and misdirection he'd used to protect her from the truth about what his research had become. He couldn't meet her eyes, couldn't bear to see the moment when love turned to betrayal, when she realized that her husband had brought this nightmare into their lives.

The leader stepped closer still, now only four feet from the couch, his shadow blotting out the thin daylight that spilled through the cabin's windows. When he spoke, his voice carried the casual authority of someone accustomed to controlling conversations through the implicit threat of violence.

"So, Doctor Carter, let's cut through the pretense and get to the heart of the matter. Was it the money? A massive payday from some competing defense contractor? Or was it something else—ideology, perhaps? A misguided sense of moral superiority?"

"No money," Carter said, his voice barely above a whisper. "Doing the right thing doesn't have a price tag. Some principles aren't for sale."

The man's mouth twitched in a humorless smile. "How refreshingly naive. Doing anything has a price, Doctor. And a cost. Something you're experiencing in real time right now. The question is whether your principles are worth the suffering of the people you claim to love." He gestured toward Laura and Miles without taking his eyes off Carter. "From where I stand, it doesn't look like you made the right choice."

Carter's chest tightened until breathing became a conscious effort. The weight of his decision—to expose AeroSight, to contact Voss, to try to prevent his earthquake technology from being weaponized—pressed down on him like a physical force.

"Do you even know what Kern is planning to do with it?" he asked. "What he'll do with my research? The people who'll die?"

"Not my concern," the man said with clinical detachment. "I'm what you'd call a target-specific resource. I make problems disappear permanently, and right now, you're the problem that needs solving."

"So that's it?" Carter's voice cracked with disbelief. "You're just going to kill me? Kill my family? "

The man's eyes held something colder than intent—it was inevitability.

"Killing is easy. A few pounds of pressure applied to the right trigger, and consciousness simply ... stops. I'm here to ensure that whatever you planned to leak to that reporter never sees the light of day. Your cooperation determines how much suffering precedes that inevitable conclusion."

"Let my family go," Carter said, desperation creeping into his voice despite his efforts to remain calm. "I'll do whatever you want. I'll give you everything. Just let them walk away from this."

"You don't understand, do you?" The man's tone sharpened. "The only mercy I can give you is a quick death. The pain they feel from this point forward is entirely proportional to your level of cooperation."

Carter swallowed against the bile climbing his throat. He forced himself to meet Laura's eyes—her face wet with tears, her mouth trembling with words she couldn't speak—and then Miles', whose wheezy breaths had become a drumbeat of distress.

His son's eyes held a trust that broke Carter's heart. Even now, even bound and struggling to breathe, Miles believed his father would somehow fix this.

"Who else knows?" the man asked, his interrogation taking on a practiced rhythm. "This is important, so answer carefully."

Carter latched onto the only thread of hope he could think of, the desperate lie that might buy them time. "I've got a failsafe. If anything happens to me, if I don't check in every twelve hours, a file gets sent automatically to every major news outlet in the country.

CNN, Fox, MSNBC, the Washington Post, the Times. Everything goes public."

"You're lying. Do you know how I can tell?"

Carter shook his head, feeling his face burn with shame.

The man recited the tells like reading items from a grocery list. "You looked down and to your left before speaking, your throat tightened after you said 'file,' and your right foot tapped the floor twice. Classic stress indicators. You may be good at reading geological surveys, but I've spent the better part of my career reading deception."

Having his bluff called drained what little strength Carter had left.

"So now that I know you're the only one holding the materials," the man continued, "let's make sure I get all of it. My patience is thin, and you really don't want to see what happens when it runs out." His eyes flicked toward Laura and Miles. "Children are so fragile. So many things can go wrong with their delicate little bodies."

Carter reached for the thumb drive in his pocket, the plastic edges biting into his fingers When he heard a sound from outside. The revving of an engine.

The leader's head snapped toward the front of the cabin, his entire posture shifting from the calm demeanor displayed during interrogation into something more primal. His hand moved to his sidearm's grip—not drawing, but establishing contact, ready to transition from psychological pressure to lethal force in the space between heartbeats.

"Stay put," he commanded, his voice taking on the sharp edge of tactical authority. "Don't even think about moving."

Carter noticed that the man holding his son at gunpoint had shifted slightly, looking over the top of Miles's head at the unknown variable in play.

Carter's heart hammered with desperate hope.

His gaze swept the cabin's interior with newfound urgency, looking for any advantage that might tip the scales from execution to survival. His eyes landed on the small pine end table beside the couch, where an old-fashioned oil lamp sat with its glass chimney smudged with soot from previous use.

The wick was trimmed and ready, the brass base still half full of kerosene that would burn with liquid hunger given the right spark. In the growing tension, that lamp represented possibility.

He forced his eyes away before either of the gunman noticed his interest, mind racing through calculations that had nothing to do with seismic stress patterns and everything to do with the physics of combustion and human reflexes.

"'Bout time they showed up," the team leader said, almost to himself, his voice carrying the particular satisfaction of someone whose careful planning was finally coming together. He cut a glance at his partner, then shifted his attention back to Carter with the lazy confidence of a cat watching a mouse realize it was trapped. "Don't worry, it'll all be over soon."

HATCH SLID behind the wheel of Carter's SUV and immediately pushed the seat forward, then grabbed a warped two-by-four that she'd scavenged from a debris pile along the side of the cabin.

The wood was exactly the right length to wedge between the seat frame and the accelerator pedal, transforming Carter's abandoned vehicle into a guided missile with a very specific target. She jammed the makeshift throttle in place, watching the engine's idle jump from a comfortable purr to an angry roar that would wake every creature within a mile radius.

The cabin sat less than thirty yards ahead, its rustic log construction and stone chimney looking deceptively peaceful.

Standard tactical problem with a straightforward solution: create chaos at one point while exploiting the other.

She needed to pull them to the front while she came in from the back.

Hatch twisted the steering wheel just enough to give the SUV's nose a clean shot at the cabin's front porch, then took one deep breath that tasted of pine needles and approaching violence. The kind of breath that preceded the moment when planning gave way to execution and all the careful preparation in the world came down to reflexes and training.

She shoved the gearshift into drive and felt the SUV lurch forward.

The moment her boots hit the ground, she was moving, staying low while sliding along the side of the cabin, eyes fixed on the cabin's rear corner where she hoped to change the tactical equation from hostage situation to something more closely resembling a fair fight.

The SUV hit the front porch with a thunderclap of splintering wood and buckling support beams, the front end punching through the decorative railing like it was made of toothpicks. The impact sent vibrations through the ground that she could feel in her bones, followed immediately by the explosive shatter of a picture window that had probably offered a scenic view of the mountains until it became collateral damage in the morning's violence.

Glass rained down inside the cabin like deadly confetti, each shard catching the morning light as it fell.

Hatch sprinted toward the rear of the cabin, weapon drawn, mind already shifting into the cold, analytical state that had kept her alive through a dozen similar situations. Inside that building, two professional killers were about to discover that their carefully planned operation had just become significantly more complicated.

She'd made a career of being the complication that turned other people's certainties into catastrophic miscalculations.

TWENTY

THE IMPACT HIT LIKE THUNDER. THE FRONT WALL BOWED, studs groaning, the SUV's grille punched through log and drywall until the cabin wore it like a battering ram. Steam hissed. Headlights raked the ceiling and turned every splinter into a blade of light.

Both men flinched—just a heartbeat—but it was enough.

Hatch slid through the cabin's back door like a shadow, low and fast, the broken door scraping soft across the floor. Her gun pressed out before her as she moved. The front sight post her guide as she navigated her entry.

The man posted over the family had turned his attention to the front. The muzzle came off the boy and instinctively took aim in the direction of the incoming threat, not noticing the one creeping up behind.

Hatch covered the last three steps in a blitz.

The hostage taker must've caught sight of her out of the corner of his eye. Spinning, his body shifted, exposing the boy behind him and rendering a clean shot out unpredictable.

Instead of firing her pistol, she wielded it like a hammer, driving the butt down along the man's forearm. The strike impacted the radial nerve. The reaction was immediate. A loud grunt escaped as his hand shot open, releasing the gun. It clattered under the table.

He recovered fast. Bringing his elbow around, he drove it into Hatch's sternum. Air was forced from her lungs. She staggered back as her attacker followed with an overhand right. Hatch ducked, air roaring past her ear. The man rode the miss, pivoted, and a knife flashed into his hand, blacked steel, four inches, held edge-out in a reverse grip. The transition between weapons would've made a street magician do a double take.

Hatch thrust kicked. Her boot heel connected with his hip, pushing him back.

He slashed for her ribs. But she backstepped an inch and let the blade whisper across her shirt. He followed with a stab meant to punch through the soft parts below the sternum. Trapping his wrist with both hands, she rolled her shoulder under his forearm, and torqued. The knife hand skated past her, carving only air.

He flowed with the redirection, trying to rake the knife back across her throat. Hatch shoved his elbow, stepped inside the arc, and drove her forehead into the bridge of his nose. Cartilage crunched. His eyes watered.

She skirted the dazed man, moving behind him and snaking her left arm around his throat. Hatch brought the Glock up, pressing the muzzle into his temple. "Drop it or die."

The knife wavered before falling to the floor. The blade stuck into the hardwood.

With one under control, and now serving as a human shield, Hatch directed her attention to the next.

The other man had already found his calm. He ghosted sideways, grabbed the boy, and yanked him in front of his chest, pistol angled around the boy's shoulder. His jaw was set, eyes flat.

“Everybody stops,” he said, voice almost conversational. “Or the kid breathes through his back.”

The wife made a sound that could scrape bone. Carter moved a half step, then froze when the muzzle angled deeper into his son's shadow.

Hatch kept the first man between her and the other gunman. She held her forearm under his jaw, her biceps clamping his carotid. His blood hammered against her flexor, hot and panicked.

"Let the kid go," Hatch said, voice steady. "And maybe you two don't die here today."

"Not how this works."

Hatch eased sideways, turning her captor's bulk so the other man's muzzle had less of the boy and more of his own man.

"I'm sure we can come to a resolution that doesn't involve gun play," Hatch said, stalling, mapping angles, feeling the thud of the SUV's engine through the floor. "Lower your gun."

"Sure thing," he said. "Right after you."

The man she was holding recovered his breath and rage in the same second. He drove an elbow back at her ribs. She shifted her hips and took most of it on her belt line. Hatch grimaced, but her grip remained unchanged. He tried to drop his weight to slip the choke. She rode him down another inch and tightened the scissor of forearm to biceps.

"Dad." The boy rasped. "Dad, I—"

"Breathe, buddy," Carter said, voice breaking. "Slow. In through the nose. We're right here."

Hatch clocked the boy's wheeze—the ragged catch that said the edges of an attack were tugging at him. She needed this over within thirty seconds or less.

"It's over," she told the leader.

He slid another half step, using a toppled chair as half cover. He didn't blink. He was reading her as hard as she read him.

The man she held was less than cooperative. He clawed at her forearm and went for a head butt, trying to break her nose with the back of his skull. Leaning her chin off-center, she took it on the side of her brow—stars, but no flood. She rewarded him by shifting her grip and punishing the brachial plexus with a short, savage hammer fist.

"How about we make a deal?" the gunman said. "I kill the boy. Make you watch. Or you let my partner go. And maybe, just maybe, I let this little shit live."

"I don't like maybes. Especially when it comes to kids."

They held there, the room breathing firelight and steam and fear. In the broken window, the SUV's headlight threw a cone across the table and painted the leader's cheek in hard white. In that edge of light, Hatch saw Carter move.

Tiny. A slight shuffle. Not toward the gunman but behind him. He was sliding along the wall, hands careful, every step a prayer. His hand slowly crept to an oil lamp on the nearby shelf by the window. His eyes cut to hers.

Hatch gave him nothing back—no nod, no blink. The gunman watched for that kind of tell. Instead, she bought Carter two beats.

"You call that a shield?" she said to the leader, making her voice a needle. "You hide behind kids and think you're serving a bigger purpose? You think this is for the greater good?"

"The 'greater good' has no idea what it costs to keep them safe."

Carter's fingers wrapped the lamp's handle, lifting it slowly until it cleared the shelf.

Hatch shifted her choke hand a hair higher, just enough to make her hostage cough in a way that snapped the gunman's eyes to his own man for a split second.

"Now," Hatch said.

Carter threw the lamp.

The glass exploded against the log wall two feet from the gunman, dousing him in kerosene oil.

The gunman shielded his eyes from the flammable liquid. He fired a reflex shot. The round came out in one loud, concussive crack.

The man in her arms jerked in her chokehold as the round drilled him—high chest, left of center. She felt the impact through his back. He went slack as muscle forgot how to be muscle. His body sagged heavy and dead.

Hatch let him go the instant he gave her his weight and adjusted her Glock's aim in the same motion, firing a controlled pair at the oil-soaked gunman.

The first shot smashed glass; the second tore wood. The hostage taker abandoned his captives and was already moving—dropping his muzzle away from the boy. He dove, not for the door, but for the shattered window Hatch's first round had struck. The remaining glass blew out in a shower of glitter as he jumped through. He hit the porch hard and then vanished into the woods.

Smoke spewed from the engine, filling the interior of the cabin. Carter's wife choked out a sob, a sound of shock and relief, then pulled her son close. The acrid air added to the boy's rasp. He was now coughing uncontrollably.

Carter was already moving to them, hands shaking. "Miles—hey, buddy, eyes on me. You're okay. Laura, the nebulizer."

"It was on the table," Laura said, voice raw.

Hatch kept her pistol trained on the window a breath longer, reading air and shadow for a reappearing muzzle. Nothing. She knelt by the man she'd used as a human shield. Without looking down, she ran her fingers along the man's neck, feeling for a pulse and finding none.

She pivoted to the family. Carter fumbled the med kit open and placed the nebulizer mask on Miles's face. The little machine purred.

"I don't know who you are, but my family and I can't thank you enough for what you did." Carter said without looking up. Fear and fury made his voice sharp.

"Don't thank me yet. We're still not out of the woods." Hatch's eyes cut back to the window and the wood line beyond. "Not with one on the loose."

"What are you going to do?"

"I'm going to finish what they started."

TWENTY-ONE

HATCH SQUEEZED THROUGH THE OPENING IN THE FRONT wall of the cabin created by the Carter family's sports utility vehicle. The porch canted at an odd angle. She navigated the jutting boards to the solid ground below. Heading off in the direction of the fleeing gunman, Hatch noticed dark, wet spots in the dirt. The jagged glass of the window he departed through had opened a cut that was providing a trail for her to follow. If only that lamp had been lit, this little came of cat and mouse would be a totally different story.

Keeping her pistol high and her profile small, she moved in increments—tree to tree, rock to rock—letting the forest tell her what it had seen. Twigs had been freshly broken, cut ends bright against the dark. Boot edges depressed into the damp needles and turned earth showed where he'd slid on the incline and caught himself with his left hand.

The ground steepened. A shallow draw cut the hillside, channeling runoff and footsteps. She found a clean heel print on a bit of clay, then another, then—nothing. He'd side-stepped off the trail, doubling back under a downed fir to change the angle. Professional. Also patient.

Hatch eased past the log and felt the air change—a subtle shift you only noticed when you went quiet enough to hear your own heartbeat.

He was above her, somewhere up-slope at her two o'clock.

She dropped behind a granite shoulder as rounds snapped past, hot little wasps stitching bark and throwing splinters into her cheek. She tasted sap and dirt and metal.

"Stay where you are," he called, another controlled pair cracking the air to keep her pinned. "Let's make this quick. I've got some unfinished business back at the cabin."

She scanned left, right, and up. The slope was a puzzle of dark humps and silvered trunks. A hundred places to die from and not many to live in. Ten yards downhill, a squat rectangle broke the natural lines—an old ranger box, paint flayed by weather, a laminated trail map under the scarred plexiglass. It sat chest-high on posts, with a rusted padlock someone had forgotten to actually lock.

He sent another round into the rock two feet from her face to nudge her head back down. "You're proving to be a real pain in the ass. Kern didn't mention you had this much fight in you." He paused to click a fresh magazine into place. "I probably would have asked for a bonus."

Keep talking. She slid belly-low to the box on elbows and toes, keeping the granite between them. The padlock had a trick hinge—two taps with the butt of her pistol and it popped. Inside: a stack of paper maps in Ziplocs, a first aid tin, a coil of paracord, a damp spiral notebook with bear-sighting scrawl, and a red plastic cylinder stamped with an expiration date two seasons ago.

A flare.

Hatch palmed it and a paper map, slid them under her belly, and let the box's lid settle back down.

"You're thinking," he said. His voice had drifted ten feet right. He was moving between trees, firing single shots just wide of where she'd been to keep her pinned while he adjusted. "Thinking gets you killed."

Hatch pressed her cheek to the cold ground. She breathed once, slow and full, blowing it out between her teeth to steady her hands, and thumbed the flare's cap. It had the cheap kind of striker—pull and twist.

Above her, a pine bled sap where a bullet had gone an inch deep.

He was close. She could smell him now. Kerosene didn't just vanish. It sunk into threads, into skin and hair, a slick that lay in wait for the wrong spark.

He fired again, fast, angry this time, chewing the top corner of the ranger box. Splinters stung her neck.

"Let's stop pretending," he called. "This rescue attempt of yours is over. Death is inevitable. That I can guarantee."

Hatch slid the map up, held it at arm's length above the edge of the granite, and flicked her wrist to make it flutter like a head ducking out. His next round found it and punched a neat hole through "BEAR ROCK OVERLOOK" on the laminate.

He'd given her his position. Three trees up-slope. A notch between trunks.

"Here's how this goes," he said, voice still too calm. "You stand up. Toss the pistol. I let you walk away and you pretend that equals a win."

She slid the flare's cap back another quarter inch. The striker grit whispered.

He fired two more rounds. The first pinged rock. The second went high. He wanted her to think he'd shifted farther right than he had. Hatch didn't gift him the mistake.

She needed him to move into his own shadow. Put his oily jacket downwind of a spark. The breeze had a lazy pull down the slope, toward her. Fire climbed with wind. She needed a crosscurrent or a bounce.

Hatch scooped a stone with her left hand, palmed it, and flicked it hard to her right. It clacked against bark and rolled into needles. He answered with a reflex shot, just wide. She saw the muzzle flash through the notch. The flare's cap came free under her thumb with a tiny pop.

"Last chance," he said.

"Last chances aren't really my thing," Hatch said, and popped up.

He was thirty feet up and ten feet right from where he'd started, half-hidden in a triangle of trunks, carbine already slashing toward her. She fired her pistol twice—one at his muzzle flash to keep his head down, one at the trunk to the left to make him flinch that way. He jerked. She dragged the flare to life.

It screamed red, a harsh magnesium hiss that turned the world into emergency light. The noise ate the next half second, which was all she needed to plant her feet and throw.

She threw past him, into the thatch of pine duff piled nearby. The flare hit, bounced, and lodged against a damp log where the wind carved up the slope and back on itself, a little eddy of air that lifted sparks and pushed heat sideways.

He pivoted, cutting his eyes to the sound and then back to her. He fired a short, tight burst while stepping away from the glow.

One round bit a chunk from the ranger box post, showering her jaw with grit. Hatch slid behind the granite. The flare crackled, sending orbiting sparks into the dry pine needles.

The wind caught a thread of smoke and slid it across him. It hit his jacket. The kerosene ignited.

At first it was just a darker sheen, a wet shine that ate the red light. Then it went to orange at the seam of his sleeve where the oil lamp had struck him earlier. Flame walked up the cloth like it had been waiting there all along.

The gunman cursed, low and sharp, and slapped at it without taking his eyes off her. Another small mistake. He moved his muzzle an inch. Hatch made it cost him. She fired two shots. The first struck his hand, forcing him to choose between fire and gun. The second one hit his right thigh, where the fabric was tight across muscle.

He sank to a knee as the fire ran up his arm.

He rolled, trying to smother it. The flare hissed louder, fed by the little wind swirl, throwing heat onto the pitch and needles he'd just crushed.

The gunman fired wildly as he rolled, bullets cutting branches over her head. Hatch stayed low and let them pass, then moved left, stalking instead of charging, her pistol rock steady, her breaths metered.

As he came up on one knee, the jacket flashed bright all at once—

kerosene, cotton, and synthetic lining finding consensus. A scream erupted, raw and animalistic, as he tugged at the zipper.

She kept her sight picture centered on the space above his sternum and didn't let the past in. "Drop it."

He didn't. He collapsed to the ground as flames ravaged him.

Moving closer, rapidly closing the gap, she kicked the pistol from his hand before he could find his aim. It skittered into a patch of flame and vanished with a spit.

He lunged for her ankles—a last ugly grab, But she stepped out of it and drove the heel of her boot into his shoulder, putting him flat. He tried to roll again. The fire had him now.

He went still. The flames did not.

Hatch backed up a step, pistol still on him, and listened to the forest reassert itself. She counted to five, to ten, sight never off the ruin on the ground. When the man didn't move again, she let the muzzle drop an inch.

The flare was eating itself fast, the burning pine duff around it licking toward a patch of damp that would starve it if it didn't find a vein of resin first. She stepped in, grabbed the back edge of the log with her free hand—heat scoring her palm—and levered it forward to smother flame against soil. Sparks popped against her pants. She stamped two out with her boot, scooped the flare with a branch, and flicked it into the wet ditch carved by snowmelt. It hissed and choked and went to angry smoke.

She stood for a beat, breathing, letting her eyes map the slope again to be certain no one else had been watching and waiting through this whole exchange. The only movement was the heat shimmer and the curl of a blackened sleeve.

Hatch picked her way back to the cabin. At the edge of the yard, the wrecked SUV loomed like a toppled animal sprawled across the torn porch. Carter and his family were outside, huddled in a tight cluster. Carter sat on the dirt ground with his back to the cabin, Miles on his lap, mask cupped against the boy's face. Laura had her arms around both of them, knuckles white where she held on.

Carter looked up when Hatch walked up. The hard clench in his jaw loosened a notch when he read her eyes.

"It's finished," she said.

Laura replied, "Is he—"

Hatch looked over her shoulder where tendrils of smoke drifted up beyond the trees. She let the truth sit without details.

Miles' breath rasped under the mask, then steadied on the next cycle. Color was sneaking back into the edges of his lips.

"We can't stay here," Hatch said. "We need to put some distance between us and all of this. Others will come."

Carter swallowed. "Maybe we should call the police."

"The best chance of surviving this is lying low until we can gain some leverage. These people have reach. Right now, the best thing we can do is keep moving."

"And you're sure about this?"

Hatch scanned the tree line again. "Teams like these have to report back. When they don't, more will come."

"How do you know all of this?" Laura asked.

"Because I've been on teams like this."

"Got a vehicle?" Carter eyed the wreckage of the family SUV. "I'm no mechanic, but it doesn't look like mine's going to be of much use."

Hatch disappeared into the cabin. She rummaged in the pockets of the dead man who'd served as her human shield. She was about to give up and head out to where the crisper of the two lay when she found what she was looking for in the left cargo pocket.

"Don't think they'll be needing these anymore." Hatch brought the keys up with a jingle. "Grab what you need. Only the essentials. The quicker we're gone, the better our chances."

Carter shifted Miles to his wife and entered the cabin. He returned with a backpack. "I think this should do it."

The four made their way over to the sedan. Hatch sat in the driver's seat as Carter took care to settle his wife and son into the back seat before joining her in the front.

"You've nearly died on our behalf, and I don't even know your name."

"Hatch."

"Just Hatch?"

"I like to keep things simple."

Carter eyed the carnage and looked back at Hatch with a raised eyebrow. "I think you and I have a very different idea of what simple means."

"Life or death. I choose life." Hatch put the sedan in drive. "Doesn't get any simpler than that."

TWENTY-TWO

THE OPERATIONS CENTER HUMMED WITH THE SOUND OF machines that never slept. Banks of monitors lined the walls, their blue glow painting the room in shades of surveillance and control. Outside, gray clouds pressed against reinforced windows, filtering the afternoon light into something cold and clinical.

David Kern stood before the main display wall, hands clasped behind his back, watching data streams flow across multiple feeds. Satellite imagery. Communications intercepts. Financial transfers. The digital pulse of a world most people never knew existed.

Behind him, workstations curved in a shallow arc. Eight operators, each managing their own slice of the global chessboard. The soft click of keyboards and the whisper of air conditioning were the only sounds breaking the cathedral quiet of focused professionals doing work that didn't officially exist.

"Sir."

Kern didn't turn. He'd heard Rodriguez approach—soft-soled shoes on industrial carpet, the slight hitch in his gait from the Kandahar shrapnel he thought no one noticed.

"Alpha Team hasn't checked in," Rodriguez said. "They're overdue."

Now Kern turned. Rodriguez held a tablet, his face carefully neutral. Good operator. Never showed stress even when the math started going wrong.

"Define overdue."

"Twenty-two minutes past their last comm window."

Kern's jaw tightened. In his line of work, twenty-two minutes could mean equipment failure. Could mean operational security protocols. Could mean a team was lying in pieces at the bottom of a Virginia ravine.

He followed Rodriguez to his workstation, noting the clean desk, the precisely arranged monitors. It was why Kern had poached him from Raytheon three years ago.

"Don't waste time with calls," Kern said, settling into the chair beside him. "Bring up any drone assets in the area."

Rodriguez's fingers moved across the keyboard with practiced efficiency. Windows cascaded across his main monitor. Flight paths appeared as thin green lines over topographic maps. Asset positions updated in real time.

"Got one," Rodriguez said. "Reaper. Running surveillance on a suspected drug route about twelve klicks northeast of the target zone."

"Divert it," Kern said, his voice cutting like a blade.

"Sir, that's a DEA operation. If we pull their bird—"

"I said divert it."

Rodriguez nodded and opened a secure channel. His voice took on the flat professionalism of a man accustomed to giving orders that couldn't be questioned. "Control, this is Override Seven. Requesting immediate asset reallocation per National Security Directive."

The response crackled through speakers. "Override Seven, you are cleared for asset control. Transferring to your grid."

The main display shifted. Camera feed from thirty thousand feet, the mountains spread below like a relief map made of shadow and stone. The image quality was crisp enough to read license plates.

"Target coordinates," Kern said.

Rodriguez inputted the cabin location. The camera began its automated swing. The mountains slid past in a silent ballet of surveillance technology.

Then, the cabin appeared on screen.

Kern leaned forward. The SUV was there—Samuel Carter's vehicle buried nose-first in what had been the front porch. Splintered wood radiated from the impact like a lumber explosion frozen in time. Smoke still curled from a blackened patch of ground near the tree line.

"Close in," Kern ordered.

The camera zoomed. Details sharpened. Broken glass caught the afternoon light. The SUV's rear wheels hung suspended over the porch foundation, the whole scene looking like a child's toys scattered by an angry god.

"Thermal overlay," Kern said.

The image shifted to infrared. Heat signatures bloomed in false color—the SUV's engine still warm, the smoldering remains of the fire, and there, thirty meters up the slope, the cooling corpse.

Kern stared at the screen. His team was now nothing more than a heat signature fading to ambient temperature.

"Damn it," Kern muttered.

He stood silent. Around him, the operations center continued its quiet hum. Other screens showed other operations—arms shipments in Yemen, oil platforms in the Gulf, a dozen different ways of applying force to achieve objectives.

But this screen showed failure. And failure, in Kern's experience, was just another form of data. Something to be analyzed, understood, and corrected.

"It's time to test Project Rift in the real world."

Rodriguez's fingers paused over his keyboard. "Sir, I didn't think it was fully operational."

Kern's smile was thin as a razor blade. "That's why I said test."

He moved to Rodriguez's shoulder, pointing at a secondary monitor. "Pull telemetry on Thorne's vehicle. I want a GPS lock on it—now."

"Already pulling it up." Rodriguez opened another window. Lines of code scrolled past—vehicle identification numbers, GPS coordinates, engine diagnostics. "Got it. The car's still transmitting. Last known position matches the cabin area."

"Good." Kern straightened. "And Rodriguez?"

"Sir?"

"Prep the Rift system. I want targeting solutions for the entire area. One-mile radius from Thorne's last position."

Rodriguez's hands slowed. "Sir, that's ... that would be a significant seismic event. If there are civilians—"

"There won't be any civilians. Trust me on that."

He walked away from the workstation, leaving Rodriguez to his calculations. The secure corridor beyond the operations center was quieter, lined with brushed steel and recessed lighting that made everything look like the inside of a very expensive coffin.

Kern pulled his phone from his inner jacket pocket. Encrypted. Untraceable. The kind of device that cost more than most people's cars and disappeared from inventory lists the day it was manufactured.

He dialed a number he knew by heart.

Two rings. Then: "Tell me it's all taken care of."

Harlan's voice carried that blend of arrogance and anxiety that came from spending decades believing his money could solve any problem.

Kern paused before responding. "There's been ... a slight hiccup."

The silence on the other end stretched for three heartbeats. When Harlan spoke again, his voice had dropped to the register he used for threatening committee witnesses.

"A hiccup?"

"I'm handling it. As we speak." Kern began walking, his footsteps echoing softly in the corridor. "Carter will be buried by his own design—and with him, all of our problems."

"What the hell does that mean?"

"It means, Congressman, that sometimes the most elegant solutions are also the most poetic." Kern reached the end of the corridor, where floor-to-ceiling windows looked out over the Potomac. The river moved past with the same indifference it had shown for centuries—carrying secrets and bodies with equal efficiency. "Carter wanted to expose the dangers of induced seismic activity. I'm about to give him a front-row seat."

Another pause. Then Harlan's voice, smaller now, "You're really going to use it?"

"Don't sound so worried. Look at how things turned out for us in Riverton."

"Speaking of. What about the woman?"

Kern's reflection stared back at him from the window glass—calm, composed, a man in complete control of his world. "She'll be buried with the rest of them."

He ended the call and pocketed the phone. Behind him, the operations center hummed with renewed activity. Rodriguez would be running calculations, preparing targeting solutions, calibrating equipment that had cost the taxpayers two billion dollars and didn't officially exist.

Sometimes, Kern reflected, the best way to bury the truth was literally.

TWENTY-THREE

THE MOUNTAIN ROAD UNWOUND BENEATH THEM LIKE A dark ribbon. Hatch drove the sedan procured from the dead hit men, handling the curves as they came. Hatch kept her hands light on the wheel, carving a path through the thin fog. In the rearview mirror, the cabin had long since vanished behind timber and stone, but the smell of the burned man still clung to her clothes.

Miles sat pressed against the far window in the backseat next to his mother, his small frame rigid with the kind of stillness that came after violence. His breathing had steadied—the nebulizer had done its work—but his eyes held that glassy look of a kid who'd seen too much too early.

"You doing okay back there, Miles?" Hatch asked, adjusting the mirror to catch his reflection.

He nodded without looking away from the window. "I guess."

"You were very brave today. Most kids would have fallen apart."

"Not like you." His voice was small, uncertain. "Don't you get scared?"

Hatch slowed for a tight curve, letting the question settle between them. In the passenger seat, Carter turned slightly, waiting for her answer.

"Of course I do," she said. "That's the truest measure of bravery—moving forward against all odds, not by pretending fear doesn't exist, but by embracing it."

She lightened her tone, caught Carter's eye. "Your dad showed a lot of bravery too. Not sure we'd all be here if he hadn't jumped in when he did."

Her voice dropped, meant for Carter alone. "Thank you for that."

Carter's throat worked. "I just—I couldn't let them hurt my family."

Miles finally turned from the window. "Are the bad men really gone?"

"They are," Hatch said. "All of them."

The road began to level out as they descended toward the valley floor. Through the windshield, the sky was shifting. The first fat drops of rain hit the glass, scattering like thrown pebbles.

Carter shifted in his seat, reality reasserting itself. "So what's the plan?"

"First, we ditch this ride and grab my Jeep. Too many people might be looking for this vehicle," Hatch said, flicking on the wipers as the rain picked up. "Then we put more distance between ourselves and that cabin.

Hatch said, flicking on the wipers as the rain picked up.

"And after that?"

"Get you and your family somewhere safe until we can put your evidence into the right hands."

Carter was quiet for a moment. "But Ethan Voss is dead."

"Is there anyone else you trust? Someone who'd have the reach to get this story out?"

Carter rubbed his jaw, thinking. "Maybe. Voss worked for Mario Parsons at the *Tribune*. Voss said that Parsons was the kind of editor who still believes journalism can change the world. He backed Ethan through some hairy stories in the past. Hopefully, he'll do the same for us now."

Laura leaned forward from the back seat. "Sam, are you sure about this? Getting more people involved?"

"We can't fight this alone," Carter said. "We need someone with a platform. Someone who can get the story out before it's too late."

Hatch took another curve, the sedan's tires whispering on wet asphalt. Ahead, the familiar glow of Pete's Diner materialized through the rain, neon sign flickering against the gray morning.

"We'll stop here," she said, pulling into the lot. "I'll grab some food while you make the call."

The parking lot was different from the night before. Raff's Peterbilt was gone, along with most of the long-haul rigs. Just a few scattered cars and the persistent smell of diesel and bacon grease.

She killed the engine and pocketed the keys. "Five minutes. Keep the doors locked."

Inside, the diner buzzed. Darlene was nowhere in sight. A different waitress worked the counter. She glanced up as Hatch entered, coffee pot already in hand.

"What can I get you?"

"Coffee to go. Three cups. A carton of milk. And whatever you've got that travels well."

"Got some breakfast sandwiches made up. Egg, cheese, sausage. They're pretty good."

"I'll take four of those."

While the waitress assembled the order, Hatch kept one eye on the parking lot through the rain-streaked windows. Carter was on his phone, leaning forward intently, one hand gesturing as he spoke. Laura had moved to the middle seat, close enough to hear the conversation, Miles curled against her side.

The waitress returned with a cardboard carrier and a paper bag. Hatch paid the tab in cash and was out the door.

Hatch left a twenty and headed back into the rain. By the time she reached the sedan, Carter was ending his call.

"How'd it go?" she asked, sliding behind the wheel.

"He's shaken up about Ethan. Mad as hell." Carter pocketed his phone. "But he wants to meet. He'll run the story if I can prove what I'm claiming."

"Where?"

"His office. Downtown. He said he'd wait for us."

Hatch started the engine. "We'll need to switch vehicles first," she said, pulling around to the back of the diner where her Jeep waited. "Can't roll into the nation's capital in a dead man's car."

They transferred their gear quickly, the rain coming harder now, drumming against the diner's metal roof. Hatch opened the hidden compartment behind her rear wheel well and retrieved her backup Glock, checking the action before sliding it into the console.

Miles watched the gun disappear with wide eyes. "Are we going to need that?"

"Hopefully not," Hatch said, settling behind the wheel of her Jeep. "But better to have it and not need it than the other way around."

She left the sedan parked in the shadows behind the diner, keys on the dashboard. Someone would find it eventually, but they'd be long gone by then.

The Jeep started. Hatch adjusted the mirrors, checked her sight lines, and pulled back onto the highway.

"D.C. it is," she said, windshield wipers beating a steady rhythm against the rain.

Behind them, Pete's Diner receded into the gray morning, just another waypoint in a journey that was far from over. Ahead, the highway stretched toward the capital, where Mario Parsons waited with the power to turn their evidence into a weapon that could bring down David Kern.

If they could get there in one piece.

The rain fell harder, and somewhere in the distance, thunder rolled across the mountains.

TWENTY-FOUR

DAVID KERN STOOD BEFORE THE WALL OF MONITORS, watching data streams update in real time. The operations center had taken on the focused intensity of a mission in progress—operators bent over their keyboards, voices lowered to the clipped professionalism of people who understood that lives hung in the balance of their calculations.

Rodriguez looked up from his workstation, stylus poised over a tablet displaying topographic overlays. "Sir, we've got a lock on the team leader's vehicle."

"Show me."

The main display shifted to satellite imagery, the camera pulling back to reveal a wider area of Virginia's Blue Ridge. A red dot pulsed steadily against the green backdrop of forest and winding roads.

"GPS tracker's still active," Rodriguez said. "Vehicle's stationary. Looks like it's behind some kind of commercial building."

Kern leaned closer, studying the image. "Zoom in."

The camera adjusted, bringing the building into sharp focus. A low, sprawling structure with a neon sign. He panned out to the parking lot. The sedan sat in the shadows behind the building, nearly invisible except for the infrared signature of its cooling engine.

"It's a truck stop," Rodriguez said. "Place called Pete's Diner."

"How long has it been stationary?"

Rodriguez checked his logs. "Fifty-two minutes."

Too long for a simple fuel stop. Kern's jaw tightened as he processed the implications. Thorne's team had been eliminated, but their vehicle had somehow ended up at a diner nearly ten miles from Samuel Carter's cabin. Which meant someone had driven it there. Someone who was now gone.

"Pull up traffic cameras for the area," Kern ordered. "I want to see what vehicles have left that location in the last hour."

Rodriguez's fingers flew across his keyboard. Multiple windows opened, showing grainy footage from highway cameras scattered throughout the region. The timestamps rolled backward as he searched for relevant movement.

"There," he said, highlighting one feed. "Jeep. Left the diner approximately thirty-eight minutes ago. Heading northeast on Route 522."

The image was distant, blurry, but clear enough to show four occupants. Kern watched the Jeep disappear around a curve, already knowing what he would find when Rodriguez enhanced the image.

"Run facial recognition on the driver."

The computer churned for several seconds, comparing pixels against known databases. Then a match appeared: Rachel Hatch. The woman who had single-handedly destroyed Kern's Riverton operation. The woman who should have been dead at the bottom of a ravine with the rest of Thorne's team.

"Son of a bitch," Kern muttered.

"Sir?"

"She's alive. The woman from Riverton. Which means she has Carter. And his family. And whatever evidence he planned to leak."

Rodriguez looked up from his screen. "Orders, sir?"

Kern moved to the tactical display, where a three-dimensional map of Virginia spread before him like a digital war room. He traced possible routes with his finger—highways, back roads, the logical paths someone would take when trying to reach Washington, D.C. with sensitive information.

"They'll head for the city," he said, thinking aloud. "Carter made contact with someone. A journalist, most likely. Someone who can disseminate what he's carrying."

"Intercept teams?"

"No." Kern shook his head. "Too risky. She's proven she can handle conventional tactics." His finger stopped on a particular section of the map, where a thin line represented a two-lane highway cutting through a ridge. "What's the optimal deployment location for Project Rift along their probable route?"

Rodriguez pulled up a different overlay—geological surveys, seismic stress points, structural vulnerability assessments. The data painted a picture of a landscape honeycombed with fault lines and unstable rock formations.

"Here," Rodriguez said, highlighting a section of highway. "Hollowback Ridge Tunnel. Route 214, about forty miles northeast of their current position."

"Tell me about it."

"Built in 1954. Seven hundred and fifty feet long, cuts through layered shale with limestone deposits. Minimal seismic reinforcement —they didn't have modern earthquake standards when it was constructed." Rodriguez pulled up engineering reports and architectural surveys. "Perfect geological conditions for a controlled collapse."

Kern studied the data, mind already working through the implications. A tunnel collapse would be devastating but localized. Officially, it would look like a tragic geological event—old infrastructure finally succumbing to natural stress. The kind of accident that made headlines for a day before being forgotten.

"Time to target?"

Rodriguez ran calculations based on traffic patterns and driving speeds. "Assuming they maintain current heading and velocity ... approximately ninety minutes."

"And our deployment window?"

"Rift system can be online and calibrated within sixty minutes.

We'll have plenty of time to lock onto their exact position before they enter the tunnel."

Kern nodded slowly. It was elegant in its simplicity. Carter wanted to expose the dangers of induced seismic activity—he would die experiencing them firsthand. The irony was almost poetic.

"Prep the system," he ordered. "I want targeting solutions for the entire ridge structure. When they enter that tunnel, I want them buried so deep it'll take archaeologists to find them."

Rodriguez hesitated. "Sir, there may be other traffic in the area. Civilian vehicles."

"Collateral damage." Kern's voice carried no emotion. "The greater good sometimes requires smaller sacrifices."

"Understood, sir."

The operations center shifted into high gear around them. Technicians ran system diagnostics. Satellite feeds repositioned to provide real-time monitoring of the target zone. The digital machinery of state-sanctioned murder hummed to life with the efficiency of a Swiss timepiece.

Kern returned to the main display, watching the red dot that represented Rachel Hatch's Jeep moving steadily toward its appointment with geological destiny. In ninety minutes, Hatch would discover what happened when you interfered with forces beyond your comprehension.

Samuel Carter would learn that some secrets were worth killing for.

David Kern would finally close the book on the most persistent thorn in his side.

The mountain would do the rest.

TWENTY-FIVE

THE JEEP'S ENGINE HUMMED, HEADLIGHTS CARVING A steady path through the Virginia hills. Rain drummed against the windshield in a hypnotic rhythm. In the backseat, Laura and Miles had finally succumbed to exhaustion. The food had helped—warm protein and carbohydrates working their magic on bodies that had burned through adrenaline like rocket fuel. Laura's arm draped protectively over Miles, who was curled against her side with the boneless sleep of childhood.

Carter watched them in the rearview mirror, his face etched with bone-deep worry. Dark circles shadowed his eyes, and his hands trembled where they rested on his knees.

"It'll all be over soon," Hatch said quietly, keeping her voice low enough not to wake the sleepers and noting how Carter's eyelids drooped despite his obvious efforts to stay alert. "That adrenaline dump from earlier is like a knockout drug. Your body's trying to recover from what it just went through."

Carter shook his head. "I don't think I'll ever be able to sleep again."

"You'd be surprised what you can get used to." Hatch's voice carried the weight of experience. "The human mind has an amazing capacity for adaptation. Even for the worst scenarios."

Carter studied her profile, his gaze settling on the exposed scar that twisted up her right arm, disappearing under her sleeve. "You military?"

"Used to be."

"So what are you now? Some kind of mercenary?"

Hatch let out a short laugh, more air than humor. "I'm just a civilian now."

Carter frowned, confusion creasing his brow. "But you being here ... those guys seemed to know who you were."

"Got duped into being there by one of Kern's bedfellows." The words came out flat, matter-of-fact. "Wrong place, wrong time. Story of my life lately."

Carter nodded slowly, still not putting all the pieces together. "Well, my family and I are lucky you were there." He paused, studying her face. "Why help us now? You could have just walked away."

Hatch was quiet for a moment, considering her answer. Rain sheeted across the windshield. She leaned forward to see the road markings.

"My father taught me to help good people who've been wronged," she said finally. "You folks seem like you fit the mold."

She glanced at him, her expression hardening. "He also taught me to punish those responsible for causing them harm. And with Kern, I plan to get my pound of flesh."

"How do you know Kern anyway?"

"Crossed paths with him recently. Or rather, crossed paths with his plans, in a town called Riverton."

Carter's eyes widened. "When I saw that on the news, knowing what I know about Kern, and seeing that AeroSight was getting a big contract out of the calamity ... I knew there was more to the story."

"I saw firsthand the lengths he'll go to," Hatch said, her voice carrying a cold edge. "I plan to ensure I stop him in his tracks."

Carter reached into his jacket and pulled out the thumb drive, holding it up for her to see. "Get this to the right people. and it'll bury Kern for good."

"What exactly do you have on there?"

Carter was quiet for a moment. "My research. The breakthrough I made in fault line pressure relief technology." He turned the drive over in his fingers. "See, most people think earthquakes are just random acts of nature. But they're not. They're the result of stress building up along fault lines over decades, sometimes centuries."

He leaned forward, his scientist's passion overcoming his exhaustion. "I developed a way to create controlled micro-fractures—essentially tiny earthquakes—that relieve that pressure gradually instead of letting it build to catastrophic levels. Think of it like ... controlled burns in forest management. You create small fires to prevent massive wildfires."

Hatch nodded. "Sounds like it could save a lot of lives."

"That was the idea. San Francisco, Los Angeles, the entire Pacific Northwest—they're all sitting on ticking time bombs. My technology could defuse those bombs, release the pressure safely over time instead of waiting for 'the big one.'" His voice grew quieter. "What I didn't see was the weaponized potential."

"But Kern did."

"Exactly. Instead of using it to prevent disasters, he figured out how to cause them for his own benefit. Turn my pressure-relief system into a weapon that could trigger earthquakes on command."

Hatch felt a chill that had nothing to do with the mountain air. "He could assassinate foreign entities, collapse infrastructure, make it all look like natural disasters."

"That's just the beginning." Carter's voice dropped to barely above a whisper. "There are plenty of fault lines stateside. Might be a great way to leverage power domestically too. If someone pushes back against his policy agenda ... how about he shakes things up in California? Or triggers a 'natural disaster' that requires his company's services to clean up?"

The pieces clicked into place with sickening clarity. Kern wasn't just building a weapon—he was building a tool for absolute control. The power to reshape the world from the ground up.

"Jesus," Hatch breathed.

"The files on that drive contain everything—technical specifications, test results, communication logs with Kern's people. Enough to prove that he's turned earthquake prevention into earthquake creation."

They drove in silence for several minutes, both lost in the implications. Finally, Hatch glanced at the clock on the dashboard.

"We've got about an hour before we reach D.C.," she said. "Might as well try to get some shuteye. Sleep when you can—old military rule."

Carter nodded and shifted in his seat, rolling slightly toward the window. Within minutes, his breathing had deepened, exhaustion finally claiming him.

Hatch drove on through the rain, alone with her thoughts and the weight of what they were carrying. In the backseat, the Carter family slept the sleep of people who had survived the unthinkable. Her plan was to make sure the man responsible faced the consequences of his actions.

TWENTY-SIX

THE TUNNEL ENTRANCE LOOMED AHEAD LIKE AN OPEN mouth preparing to swallow them whole, its dark throat disappearing into the bowels of Hollowback Ridge. A weathered yellow sign flickered past in the steady rain, its reflective surface catching their headlights for a moment before vanishing into the rearview mirror:

HOLLOWBACK RIDGE TUNNEL EST. 1954

NO TRUCKS OVER 12' CLEARANCE

This tunnel had been carved through solid rock using the engineering standards of the Eisenhower era, when men had built things to last forever but hadn't accounted for enemies who could turn the earth itself into a weapon.

Hatch eased off the accelerator as they passed into the throat of the mountain, the world outside vanishing like a door closing on daylight. The familiar Virginia landscape of forest and farmland was replaced by walls of aging concrete stained dark with decades of mineral runoff that painted abstract patterns like geological hieroglyphs no one alive could read.

Sodium lights mounted every fifty feet cast pools of sickly yellow illumination that barely pushed back the shadows between them, creating a strobing effect as they drove deeper into the mountain's belly. The lighting was institutional, harsh, the kind of clinical brightness that belonged in morgues and government basements rather than places where living people were supposed to travel.

Water dripped from hairline cracks in the ceiling, each drop echoing in the enclosed space like a slow, irregular heartbeat that marked time with the patient rhythm of geological processes beyond human control. The air tasted of wet stone and motor exhaust, thick enough to feel on the tongue, carrying the mineral tang of deep earth and the accumulated exhalations of decades of passing vehicles.

Steel I-beams ran along the tunnel's length like the ribs of some massive, fossilized creature. Massive supports were bolted into the rock face every twenty feet. The industrial design spoke to an era when American engineering was synonymous with permanent solutions to permanent problems. They looked solid, reassuring—the kind of over-engineering that had built the interstate highway system and put men on the moon.

Rust streaked their surfaces like old blood, the inevitable victory of time and moisture over human ambition, but the metal itself remained thick and unyielding. These beams had been designed to hold up mountains, and they wore their responsibility with the stolid indifference of structures that had never failed in their duty.

The Jeep's engine note changed as they penetrated deeper into the tunnel, the sound echoing off the concrete walls in a low growl that multiplied and distorted in the confined space. Acoustic physics turned their passage into something primal, the mechanical heartbeat of civilization intruding into a space that had existed in darkness for geological ages before humans learned to make fire.

Halfway through the tunnel's length, the sound started.

A low frequency hum, barely perceptible at first, reverberating within Hatch's bones rather than her ears. A vibration that seemed to come from the mountain itself, as if some vast machine buried deep in the granite core had stirred to life after decades of dormancy.

The kind of sound that made your teeth ache and your inner ear rebel against sensory input that had no place in the normal spectrum of human experience.

Then it grew.

The hum became a throb, deep and rhythmic, like the heartbeat of something vast and ancient that had been sleeping beneath the earth since before continents had learned their current shapes. The steering wheel vibrated under Hatch's hands with a frequency that traveled through her arms and settled in her chest like a second pulse competing with her own biological rhythms. She slowed the Jeep.

Dust sifted from the ceiling cracks, particles dancing in the headlight beams like snow that had been waiting seventy years to fall. The concrete overhead, which had seemed so solid moments before, now revealed its age in the form of stress fractures that spread with visible speed across surfaces that had been engineered to last forever.

Carter's eyes snapped open in the passenger seat, his body jerking from the involuntary sleep of emotional exhaustion into the sharp awareness of professional terror. For a moment he looked confused, disoriented by the strange acoustics of the tunnel and the quality of artificial light that made everything look like an industrial fever dream.

Then his face went white.

"Oh, God," he whispered, his voice barely audible over the growing mechanical symphony. "That's—that's the harmonic frequency. They're using the Rift system."

The words hit Hatch like physical blows, confirmation of what she'd already suspected but hoped against. Kern hadn't just tried to eliminate them through conventional violence. He'd decided to erase them from existence using the very technology Carter had developed to save lives.

The world exploded.

Ahead of them, the tunnel exit collapsed with a sound like the earth itself screaming in agony, as if the mountain had been wounded by forces beyond its ability to comprehend or resist. Tons of rock and concrete crashed down in a symphony of destruction that echoed through the tunnel like the death rattle of a geological giant, sealing the way they'd come in a choking cloud of dust and debris that turned the air into a gray soup of pulverized stone.

The sodium lights flickered once, twice, then died in sequence, plunging half the tunnel into absolute darkness.

"Hold on!" Hatch slammed on the brakes with enough force to lock the wheels, threw the Jeep into reverse, and floored the accelerator in a desperate gambit to turn physics into prayer.

The engine roared with a mechanical fury, tires shrieking against wet concrete as they rocketed backward through the tunnel.

The mountain came down. The entrance to the tunnel disappeared.

Rock poured from the ceiling like a gray waterfall, chunks the size of refrigerators and small cars crashing down to block their escape. The exit vanished behind a wall of stone and twisted metal, the tunnel's mouth sealed as completely as if it had never existed, as if the outside world had been nothing more than a shared hallucination.

They were buried alive beneath forty feet of Virginia mountain, entombed in a space that had suddenly transformed from a passage to a crypt.

TWENTY-SEVEN

THE JEEP SKIDDED TO A STOP WITH THE METALLIC SHRIEK of abused brake pads, headlights now the only source of light in what had become their tomb. The sudden silence that followed the collapse was almost worse than the noise had been—the kind of quiet that belonged to graves and abandoned places where sound went to die.

In that suffocating stillness, Hatch could hear nothing but the settling of debris like the breathing of some vast creature, and the rapid, panicked breathing of three civilians trying not to surrender to claustrophobic terror.

Laura jerked awake in the backseat, disoriented and terrified, her maternal instincts kicking in before her conscious mind had fully processed the scope of their situation. "What—Sam, what's happening? Why is it so dark?"

Miles started to cry, the sound thin and frightened in the enclosed space, carrying the desperation of a child whose world had just become incomprehensibly dangerous. "I can't breathe! Mom, I can't—the air feels heavy!"

"It's okay, baby," Laura said, though her own voice shook with the effort of maintaining calm. "It's okay. Mommy's here."

Carter stared at the debris choking both ends of the tunnel.

"They used it," he said, barely audible above the sound of his own family's terror. "They used my device. Kern turned earthquake prevention into earthquake creation, and now ..."

His voice trailed off. The thrumming sound continued, a deep bass note that seemed to come from everywhere at once, vibrating through the steel and stone that surrounded them. More dust sifted from the ceiling like poisonous snow. Hairline cracks spread across the concrete overhead like spider webs spun by some patient arachnid that measured its work in structural failure rather than silk.

"Carter," Hatch said, her voice cutting through the fear with a sharp edge. "I need options. Now."

He scanned the tunnel walls, reading the rock face like a book written in stone and pressure.

"The beams," he said. "Those steel I-beams—they're anchored into granite. This whole ridge is granite core with shale overlay." He pointed to a section of wall where dark stone showed through gaps in the concrete lining. "The granite won't collapse like the shale. It's been here for millions of years."

"What are you saying?"

"Get us next to the support beams. The ones anchored deepest into the granite face." His voice grew stronger as the scientist in him took over. "If this tunnel comes down—when it comes down—the granite will hold. The beams will create a pocket. A void. Space where we might survive long enough for rescue."

Hatch was already moving before he finished speaking, maneuvering the Jeep toward the heaviest cluster of support beams. Steel pillars thick as ancient trees rose around them, their bases disappearing into solid rock that had witnessed the rise and fall of mountain ranges.

The thrumming intensified, the artificial earthquake gaining power as the Rift system found its resonant frequency and began to teach the mountain new ways to fail. The cracks in the ceiling widened with visible speed, concrete that had been designed to last centuries giving way to forces that belonged to the deep earth rather than the shallow world where humans built their temporary structures.

A chunk of concrete the size of a bowling ball crashed down ten feet ahead of them, shattering into deadly fragments that bounced off the Jeep's hood like geological shrapnel.

"Hurry," Carter breathed.

Hatch gunned the engine, racing toward the granite section Carter had identified while above them the mountain groaned with the sound of geological forces too vast for human comprehension.

"There!" Carter pointed to a section where three massive I-beams formed a triangle of steel. "Get us between those supports!"

Hatch spun the wheel, sliding the Jeep into the narrow space between the beams where small mistakes had large consequences. Steel rose around them like the ribs of some massive beast, bolted deep into granite that had withstood the rise and fall of civilizations without yielding an inch to time or weather.

The ceiling cracked with a sound like gunshots fired in rapid succession, each fracture releasing decades of accumulated stress in a display of structural failure that belonged in engineering textbooks rather than lived experience. Water began pouring through the fissures—not the steady drips they'd heard before, but streams that turned the air misty and made the concrete overhead glisten like the roof of a cave.

"Everyone down!" Hatch shouted. "Get below the windows! Protect your heads!"

Laura pulled Miles down with her, shielding his small body with her own while whispering reassurances that neither of them believed but both desperately needed. Carter ducked low, hands over his head, mind still calculating stress loads and failure points even as his world collapsed around him in the most literal sense possible.

Hatch killed the engine and dove across the seat just as the mountain came down with the finality of geological time compressed into human seconds.

The world ended in noise.

Concrete and stone crashed down with the force of an avalanche channeled through artificial constraints, tons of debris hammering the steel beams above them with impacts that rang like bell strikes in a cathedral of destruction. The I-beams held—barely—their steel frames vibrating with harmonics that belonged to the deep places where tectonic plates ground against each other in slow-motion violence.

The beams formed a crude cage that kept the worst of the collapse from crushing them, but the sound was overwhelming—a symphony of destruction that included the scream of tortured metal, the crash of falling stone, and the deep, bass roar of a mountain settling into a new configuration that would be visible from orbit.

Then, silence.

Darkness, absolute and complete, pressed against them. The headlights had died with the engine, leaving them in a black so total it had weight and substance, the kind of darkness that existed in deep caves and ocean trenches where light had never penetrated.

They were alive. The Jeep took a pounding, crumpling under the weight of shifted earth. Trapped beneath forty feet of debris in a space roughly the size of a subway car, but alive.

For now.

The air they had would last perhaps an hour if they were careful. Maybe two if they were lucky and the laws of physics decided to be generous.

In the suffocating darkness, Hatch could hear Miles crying softly and Laura whispering comfort that tasted of desperation. Carter's breathing came in the shallow pants of someone calculating their remaining time in terms of oxygen consumption rather than hope.

TWENTY-EIGHT

THE OPERATIONS CENTER HAD GONE DEAD QUIET EXCEPT for the steady hum of electronics and the soft click of Rodriguez's fingers on his keyboard. Every screen showed different angles of the same devastation—satellite feeds, drone cameras, thermal imaging—all focused on what had been Hollowback Ridge Tunnel.

David Kern stood before the main display, watching the dust cloud settle over tons of collapsed rock and twisted metal. Where the tunnel entrance had been, only a scar remained—a jagged wound in the mountainside that looked like it had been there for centuries.

"Beautiful," he murmured.

Rodriguez glanced up from his workstation, stylus paused over his tablet. "Sir?"

"Nothing, Rodriguez. Just appreciating the elegance of properly applied force."

The main screen shifted to thermal imaging, false colors painting the destruction in shades of cooling debris. No heat signatures. No movement. Nothing but the slow fade of cooling rock and metal.

Kern's encrypted radio crackled to life. "Control, this is Ground Team Alpha."

"Go ahead, Alpha."

"We have visual confirmation of total structural collapse. Both tunnel entrances are completely sealed. Estimate debris depth at forty to sixty feet on the north end, thirty to forty on the south."

Kern keyed the mic. "Any chance of survival?"

A pause. Then, "Negative, sir. Even if the initial collapse didn't kill them outright, we're looking at a sealed environment approximately seven hundred feet long. Four people, limited air supply." The voice carried the clinical detachment of a man who'd calculated death before. "Oxygen deprivation will finish the job within the hour."

"What about emergency response?"

"State highway patrol will probably get the first call, but they'll have to route through county emergency management, then request heavy equipment from three different municipalities. We're talking minimum of four hours before they can even begin debris removal. More likely six to eight hours before any meaningful excavation starts."

Rodriguez looked up from his calculations. "Sir, even with immediate response, digging through that much debris ... we're talking days, not hours."

Kern nodded slowly. The mathematics were simple and unforgiving. Four people, sealed in with whatever air had been trapped during the collapse. Basic physiology said they had perhaps ninety minutes before carbon dioxide poisoning rendered them unconscious. Death would follow within hours.

By the time emergency crews broke through the outer debris field, they'd be recovering bodies, not survivors.

"Ground Team Alpha, what's your status?"

"Equipment secured and withdrawn. Site sanitized. We're Oscar Mike to extraction point."

"Copy. Good work, Alpha."

Kern set down the radio and surveyed the tactical display one final time. Red indicators marked the collapsed tunnel on the screen, overlaid with geological surveys showing the full extent of the seismic event. A controlled demolition disguised as a natural disaster—the kind of geological tragedy that made headlines for a day before being filed away under "Acts of God."

The irony wasn't lost on him. Samuel Carter, the man who'd dedicated his career to preventing earthquake disasters, had been killed by an artificially induced seismic event using his own technology. There was poetry in that. Justice, even.

"Rodriguez," Kern said, "shut it down. Archive everything under Project Lazarus protocols."

"Yes, sir." Rodriguez began closing windows, transferring data to encrypted servers. "What about the cleanup teams?"

"Standard protocol. They were never here. The equipment was never deployed. As far as anyone knows, Hollowback Ridge suffered a spontaneous geological failure—old infrastructure finally succumbing to natural stress."

"Understood, sir."

Kern took one last look at the screens showing the sealed tomb that had been Hollowback Ridge Tunnel. Somewhere beneath forty feet of rock and concrete. And his evidence—the thumb drive that could have brought down AeroSight—was buried with them, lost forever in a mountain of crumbling stone.

He turned and walked toward the exit, leaving Rodriguez to complete the digital burial. The corridor beyond was quiet, sterile, lined with the kind of corporate art that suggested power without displaying it.

At the secured exit, Kern paused to pull out his encrypted phone. He scrolled to a contact marked "H" and pressed call.

Two rings. Then Harlan's voice, tight with anxiety. "Please tell me it's finished."

"Our problem is buried," Kern said, stepping outside into the dusky Washington evening. Rain had started falling again, washing the city clean of whatever sins had been committed in secret.

"The evidence?"

"Gone. Along with everyone who might have testified to its contents."

A long exhale on the other end of the line. "Jesus, David. I still can't believe you actually did it."

"I told you I would handle it." Kern began walking toward his car, a black sedan that blended perfectly with a dozen others in the executive parking area. "Carter wanted to expose the dangers of induced seismic activity. I gave him a front-row seat to a practical demonstration."

"And the woman? Hatch?"

"Buried with the rest of them. She was good—I'll give her that. But no one's that good."

Kern reached his car and climbed behind the wheel, phone still pressed to his ear. Through the windshield, he could see the Potomac River flowing past with its usual indifference, carrying whatever secrets the current happened to find.

"What now?" Harlan asked.

"Now we move forward. The AeroSight contract proceeds as planned. Project Rift gets the funding it needs for full operational deployment. And we both get very rich while making America very safe."

"And if anyone asks questions about Carter?"

"What questions? A respected geologist was tragically killed in a natural disaster while traveling with his family. These things happen in unstable geological regions." Kern started the engine, letting it idle while he finished the call. "The beauty of this approach, Congressman, is that we used the mountain itself. No ballistics evidence. No forensics. No crime scene to investigate. Just geology doing what geology does."

"I have to admit, it's elegant."

"It's more than elegant. It's perfect." Kern put the car in gear, already thinking ahead to his next meeting, his next problem, his next solution. "By the time anyone even thinks to ask difficult questions, Hollowback Ridge will be listed as a geological survey curiosity. Another example of aging infrastructure succumbing to natural forces."

He ended the call and pulled out of the parking area, merging into D.C. traffic with smooth confidence. In the rearview mirror, the AeroSight building receded into the twilight, its glass facade reflecting nothing but sky and possibilities.

TWENTY-NINE

HATCH'S FIRST AWARENESS WAS THE TASTE OF DUST AND the crushing weight pressing in from all sides, as if the mountain itself had decided to embrace them with the kind of affection that broke bones and stopped breathing.

Darkness surrounded them. Not the soft darkness of a moonless night or the comfortable black of a bedroom with curtains drawn, but the brutal black of being buried alive—the kind of darkness that had weight and substance, that pressed against your eyeballs and made you question whether sight was something you'd imagined. Air thick with powdered concrete and the metallic tang of blood, her own blood, from wounds she couldn't yet catalog but could taste in the back of her throat.

Her ears rang with a high whine that might have been tinnitus from the massive acoustic trauma of a mountain collapsing, or the settling of tons of debris overhead, the sound of gravity and geology reaching some new equilibrium that included her body as part of the structural calculations.

She tried to move and discovered she was wedged between the Jeep's seat and something that had once been the dashboard but now resembled an abstract sculpture created by forces that understood compression better than aesthetics. Metal groaned somewhere above her—not the healthy flex of engineered materials under load, but the tortured protest of steel being asked to bear more weight than physics allowed.

"Carter?" Hatch's voice came out as a croak, throat raw from breathing concrete dust and screaming during the collapse.

A groan answered her from somewhere to her left, followed by movement that sent more debris pattering down around them. Then Laura's voice, higher and strained with the terror of a mother who couldn't see her child: "Miles? Baby, can you hear me? Answer Mommy!"

The panic in Laura's voice cut through the post-traumatic fog in Hatch's brain like a blade, reminding her that survival was a group effort and she was currently the only one in a position to provide leadership. She forced her right arm up through the twisted wreckage, groping blindly until her fingers found the glove compartment that had somehow remained accessible despite the Jeep's transformation into a metal accordion.

The latch was warped but gave with a sharp crack that sounded unnaturally loud in their confined space. Her hand closed around the emergency flashlight—plastic casing cracked but still intact, LED bulb miraculously unbroken despite being subjected to forces that had redesigned the vehicle's interior.

She thumbed the switch and the LED light blazed to life, revealing a nightmare that made her military experience seem like pleasant daydreaming.

The Jeep looked like it had been put through an industrial trash compactor operated by someone with serious anger management issues. The roof was crushed down to window level, held in that position only by the steel I-beams that Carter had identified—massive girders that had probably saved their lives by creating a crude cage around them. Without those beams, they would have been reduced to biological paste mixed with automotive parts.

Airbags hung limp and deflated, having deployed during the initial impact and then been punctured by flying debris. The windshield was a spider web of cracks held together by safety film that had been designed to prevent exactly this kind of catastrophic failure but not the forces that could cause it.

Carter sat slumped against his door, blood trickling from a cut on his forehead that looked like it needed stitches but would have to settle for pressure and hope. His eyes were open but unfocused, probably dealing with a concussion that made thinking feel like swimming through molasses.

Laura was twisted awkwardly in the backseat, her left arm cradled against her chest in the universal posture of someone protecting broken bones. Her face was pale with shock and pain, but her eyes were clear and focused on the most important thing in her universe.

And Miles—

Miles was pressed against the far window like a small animal trying to disappear into glass and steel, eyes wide with the kind of terror that belonged in fairy tales rather than family vacations. His chest was rising and falling in rapid, shallow gasps that Hatch recognized immediately as the precursor to respiratory crisis.

"It's okay," Hatch said, forcing calm authority into her voice even though nothing was remotely okay. "We're alive. We're all alive. That's what matters right now."

She tried to reach for the hidden compartment where she had stored her Glock. But her fingers found only twisted metal and debris —the frame had been compressed beyond any hope of opening.

No weapon. No communication. No way out that she could see.

Miles' breathing grew more labored, the rapid pants of panic shifting into something more ominous—wheezing, with a tight whistle on each exhale that spoke to airways constricting under stress. His lips were taking on a faint blue tinge.

"He's having an attack," Laura said, struggling to reach him across the cramped space. "Sam, the inhaler—where's his inhaler? Where's the medical bag?"

Carter shook his head like a dog trying to clear water from its ears, attempting to force his concussed brain to provide useful information instead of the cotton-wrapped confusion that trauma had substituted for normal thought processes. "The bag. The medical bag. It was ... it was in the back. Should be ..."

They began searching frantically, hands scrambling through debris and scattered belongings that had been transformed from vacation supplies into potential life-saving equipment. Hatch kept the flashlight beam moving in a systematic pattern, trying to illuminate their search while keeping one eye on Miles, whose condition was deteriorating.

The boy's lips were blue now, his small chest working harder and harder to move air through passages that were closing like biological doors slamming shut.

"Miles," Hatch said, pulling his attention away from whatever internal catastrophe was playing out in his airways and focusing it on her face. "Look at me. Look right at me. We're going to breathe together, okay?"

She made her voice steady and authoritative, drawing on the same tone she'd used to talk wounded soldiers through shock while waiting for medevac helicopters. "Breathe in for four counts. One, two, three, four. Hold it. One, two, three, four. Now out slowly. One, two, three, four."

It was a combat breathing technique, designed to calm adrenaline responses and maintain focus under fire, but it worked just as well for panicked children whose bodies were betraying them in the worst possible circumstances. Miles tried to follow her instructions, his small chest straining against the tightness in his airways that was turning breathing from an automatic function into conscious work.

Above them, something shifted with a sound like bones breaking, followed by a shower of gravel that pattered down through the gaps in their protective cage. A reminder that the collapse wasn't necessarily finished, that they were trapped within a structure that could decide to continue falling at any moment.

"Found it!" Laura's voice cracked with relief as she held up the inhaler, the small plastic device that represented the difference between her son's survival and suffocation.

She pressed it into Miles' small hands, helping him position it properly against his lips with the practiced efficiency of someone who'd done this hundreds of times before but never under circumstances like these. Two puffs of medication, then they waited with the kind of desperate hope that parents learn when their child's life depends on chemistry and physics working the way they're supposed to.

Slowly, gradually, Miles' breathing began to ease. The whistle faded as his airways opened, allowing air to flow with something approaching normalcy. Color returned to his lips like sunrise spreading across a landscape that had been locked in winter.

Hatch swept the flashlight beam around their prison, taking inventory of their situation with the methodical approach that had kept her alive through disasters both natural and man-made. That's when she saw the water.

A thin stream was seeping from somewhere overhead—a broken runoff pipe, maybe, or groundwater finding its way through the cracks that the collapse had opened in the mountain's skin. It pooled in the depression where the Jeep's floor had buckled under the impact, already ankle-deep and rising with the patient inevitability of a tide that knew it had all the time in the world.

"We need to move," she said, the words carrying the weight of absolute necessity. "Now."

Hatch directed them to pull out their phones, hoping against hope for some connection to the outside world, but finding only the electronic equivalent of silence. No signal penetrated forty feet of rock and debris, but the devices still provided light—enough illumination to see by when combined with the flashlight.

In the combined glow of their makeshift lighting, Hatch could make out a gap in the debris pile that stretched above them like a geological ceiling. It was jagged, barely wide enough for a person to squeeze through, but it seemed to lead in the direction where the tunnel entrance had been before the mountain decided to redecorate.

"That way," she said, pointing toward their only hope of escape. "Single file. I'll go first, Carter brings up the rear. Stay close, stay quiet, and if you hear anything that sounds like more collapse, flatten yourselves against whatever surface you can find."

Getting out of the Jeep was like being born in reverse, if birth involved crawling through twisted metal and shattered glass while wearing the clothes you'd put on that morning when the world still made sense. They squeezed through gaps that physics said shouldn't exist, every movement careful and deliberate, aware that one wrong twist could trigger another collapse or open an artery that would bleed out before they could reach safety.

The steel beams groaned overhead, but they held with the stubborn integrity of American steel forged in an era when engineering had been synonymous with permanence.

The gap in the debris was worse than it had looked from inside the Jeep. Hatch had to turn sideways to fit through, rough concrete scraping her back through her jacket, chunks of rebar catching at her clothes and threatening to tear fabric that might be the only thing between her skin and the kinds of cuts that turned minor injuries into major problems.

Behind her, she could hear Laura helping Miles through the tightest spots, her voice steady and encouraging even though she was probably dealing with broken ribs and the pain that came with them. Carter pushed from behind when the boy got stuck, his hands gentle but insistent.

The water followed them with liquid persistence, lapping at their ankles and then their calves as they crawled their way through the collapsed tunnel. It was cold with the deep chill of mountain streams, carrying the taste of minerals and machine oil, probably contaminated with a dozen different chemicals that had leaked from the Jeep during its violent transformation.

The passage seemed to go on forever, a tunnel within a tunnel that led through debris fields and over obstacles that required them to crawl, climb, and squeeze in equal measure. Hatch's shoulders ached from the constant scraping against concrete and stone. The air grew hotter and thicker, loaded with dust and the smell of pulverized stone that spoke to forces powerful enough to turn solid rock into powder.

Every few feet, the debris would shift under their weight, sending new cascades of rock pattering down around them like geological rain. Each movement was a reminder that they were crawling through a structure that had failed catastrophically and might decide to fail again at any moment.

Then, the passage opened up.

They found themselves in a pocket of space just tall enough to stand in—a bubble where several large chunks of concrete had fallen in such a way as to support each other, creating an accidental room. It wasn't much, maybe eight feet across and ten feet long, but after the crushing confines of the passage, it felt like a cathedral.

The water was coming faster now, flowing through gaps in the debris with the persistence of liquid that knew it would eventually win any contest against gravity. Already up to their knees and rising steadily, turning their temporary sanctuary into a slowly filling bathtub.

Hatch played her flashlight beam over the walls, looking for any signs of weakness in the wall of dirt. She found a section that looked less solid than the rest, where smaller chunks of debris had been piled rather than fused by the incredible forces of the collapse.

She grabbed a bent piece of guardrail from the debris field, hefted it like a pickaxe, and began to attack the blockage with systematic fury.

The first swing sent vibrations up her arms that traveled all the way to her shoulders, the impact transmitting through steel and flesh with the authority of physics. The second swing chipped away a small chunk of concrete, creating a tiny avalanche of dust and pebbles. The third swing opened a hairline crack that suggested the wall might be willing to negotiate.

She kept swinging, muscles burning with the fire of sustained effort, sweat mixing with the blood from a dozen small cuts that she'd collected during their crawl through the debris field. Behind her, the Carter family huddled together in water that had risen to their waists, watching her work with the desperate hope of people who understood that her success or failure would determine whether they lived or died.

Finally, after what felt like hours but had probably been only minutes, her makeshift tool punched through the debris wall. A fist-sized hole, but enough to let a whisper of outside air flow in—proof that the surface was still there, somewhere beyond the tons of debris that separated them from daylight.

But it wasn't enough. Not nearly enough.

The water continued to rise with mechanical persistence, chest-deep now and forcing them to tilt their heads back to keep their mouths above the surface. Hatch swung the guardrail again, desperation giving her strength that came from somewhere deeper than muscle and bone, but the rock held firm with the indifference of geology.

"Come on," she muttered, raising the tool for another blow. "Come on, you bastard."

That's when she heard it.

A faint mechanical whine, barely audible over the sound of dripping water and settling debris. Her blood went cold as her mind jumped to the worst possible explanation—the Rift device, preparing to bring the rest of the mountain down on them, finishing the job.

But the sound shifted, becoming higher and more irregular. Not mechanical at all.

Yipping. Barking.

A dog.

Carter's eyes widened despite the concussion that made focusing difficult. "That's ... that's impossible."

The sound came again, closer now and more insistent. High-pitched barking with the urgency that belonged to small dogs who understood that their size made volume their only weapon against an indifferent world.

Hatch turned toward the hole she'd punched in the debris wall, hardly daring to hope but unable to suppress the possibility that maybe salvation wore fur and answered to a ridiculous name.

And where there was a dog, there could be a person. Someone who could help. Someone who could dig them out before the water claimed them all.

Someone who understood that sometimes the smallest voices carried the most important messages.

THIRTY

THE BARKING GREW LOUDER, MORE INSISTENT, ECHOING off the stone walls with an urgency that cut through the sound of rushing water. Then, the small hole went dark as something large blocked the light from outside.

"Hello?" A deep voice, muffled by forty feet of rock but unmistakable. "Anybody down there?"

Hatch's heart leaped, hope flooding through her chest like electricity. "Raff!"

"Well, I'll be damned. Hatch? That you?"

"It's me! We're trapped—four of us. Water's rising fast. We don't have much time."

Above them, she could hear Princess Mayhem's frantic yipping, the tiny dog's voice carrying a note of desperation that seemed to understand exactly what was at stake. The sound bounced off the tunnel walls, creating an echo that made the small Chihuahua sound like a pack of wolves demanding attention.

A pause, then Raff's voice came back, closer to the hole. "How much water we talking about?"

Hatch looked around their shrinking air pocket. The water was still at chest-level, inching toward their necks. Miles was standing on his tiptoes, Laura supporting him with her good arm while Carter pressed close behind them. The wet cold was bone-deep now, making their teeth chatter.

"Chest-deep and climbing. Maybe ten minutes before we're swimming."

"Alright, darlin'. Raff's gonna get you out of there. But that hole ain't near big enough. You got anything solid down there I can hook onto?"

Before Hatch could answer, she heard the rumble of a big diesel engine coming to life. The Peterbilt's exhaust note was unmistakable—deep, powerful, the sound of an engine built for serious work. The engine revved once, twice, like a mechanical beast stretching its muscles before a fight.

"What's he doing?" Carter asked, his voice tight with exhaustion and hypothermia.

"Being Raff," Hatch said, though she wasn't entirely sure herself.

A few minutes later, something metallic chinked against the stone. The tip of a tailhook appeared through the hole, attached to a heavy chain that scraped against the edges of the opening as Raff fed it through inch by inch. The steel links caught what little light penetrated their prison, glinting like silver hope descending from above.

"That's about all I can get through," he called down, his voice strained with effort. "You see if you can hook that onto something solid."

Hatch grabbed the hook, feeling its weight—serious hardware, the kind truckers used to secure loads that could kill you if they shifted wrong. The metal was cold and rough against her numb fingers, but it represented possibility, a lifeline in the literal sense.

She looked around their rapidly shrinking prison, water now lapping at her collar bones. Hatch grabbed the bent guardrail post she'd been using as a pickaxe and worked the hook around it. The metal groaned under the pressure, but the debris pile had locked the guardrail in place like concrete around a fence post. If anything could hold the weight of what Raff was planning, this was it.

"Got it!" she called up. "It's secure!"

"Y'all step back now." Raff's voice carried a note of warning. "This might get a little rough."

Hatch pressed the Carter family into the far corner, shielding Miles with her body. The boy was shivering violently now, his lips taking on a blue tinge that had nothing to do with asthma and everything to do with the mountain water that was slowly claiming their refuge.

"What's happening?" Miles whispered, his small voice barely audible over the sound of rushing water.

"Raff's going to pull us out of here," Hatch said, trying to inject confidence into her voice. "That big truck of his? It's stronger than this whole mountain."

The water was at their necks now, forcing them to stretch upward for each breath. Carter lifted Miles higher, the boy's arms wrapped around his father's shoulders. Laura pressed close beside them, her injured arm forgotten in the desperate mathematics of survival.

Above them, the chain went taut with a sharp snap that rang through their prison like a gunshot.

Then the Peterbilt's engine roared to life, eighteen wheels finding purchase on wet asphalt. Through the hole, they could hear the deep growl of the transmission downshifting, the mechanical symphony of a machine designed to haul impossible loads across impossible distances.

The guardrail post pressed into the stone, metal protesting with a high whine that set their teeth on edge. For a moment, nothing happened except the tortured sound of steel under impossible stress. The post began to bend, buckling in the middle like a giant's paperclip.

"It's not going to hold," Carter said, desperation creeping into his voice.

Then the boulder moved.

An inch at first. Then two. The chain sang with tension, transmitting the full power of forty tons of truck and trailer through steel links that had been forged to bear exactly this kind of load. Then, the massive stone lurched free with a grinding roar that filled their prison with the sound of geological surrender.

Dirt and smaller rocks avalanched down through the new opening, but the rushing water carved a path through the debris, widening the hole with each passing second. Fresh air poured in—cold, clean, alive with the promise of salvation.

"Miles first!" Hatch shouted over the chaos of falling stone and rushing water.

She boosted the boy up, his small frame fitting easily through the enlarged opening. Raff's massive hands appeared, lifting Miles the rest of the way with the gentleness of handling precious cargo. Carter was next, then Laura, both scrambling through the gap with the desperate energy of people who'd been given an unexpected reprieve from death.

Hatch grabbed the chain and started to pull herself up when the ground shifted beneath her feet. The water, now flowing freely through the new opening, had undermined the debris pile that had been their foundation. Rocks slipped and settled with the grinding protest of stone against stone. Her right ankle was pinned between two chunks of concrete that had shifted like massive puzzle pieces finding new positions.

The current was stronger now, pulling at her legs with liquid fingers that seemed determined to drag her down into the flooded tunnel. She fought to keep her head above water, pulling against the rocks with both hands, but the angle was all wrong. Physics and geology had formed an alliance against her.

The current won.

Darkness closed over her head like a liquid shroud.

Hatch held her breath and pulled against the rocks, but they held her fast with the indifferent strength of mountains. Her lungs burned, carbon dioxide building in her bloodstream like poison. Panic clawed at the edges of her vision, turning the darkness red around the edges.

After everything—surviving the cabin attack, the car crash, and the tunnel collapse—she was going to drown in six feet of muddy water while salvation waited just inches above her head.

The irony was as bitter as the mountain runoff filling her mouth.

THIRTY-ONE

PINNED INSIDE A WATERY TOMB, HATCH FOUGHT TO FREE herself. In the midst of the chaos, she thought of Daphne. She couldn't bear the thought of forcing her niece to face another tragedy. Seeing the ten-year old's face in her mind's eye gave Hatch a burst of willpower. In a final desperate effort, she dipped below the water and clawed at the rock gripping her leg.

The granite shackle gave a little but not enough to free her. The effort stripped the oxygen from her lungs. Hatch pushed her chin up past the water line to catch her breath. In a matter of minutes, she'd be completely submerged.

For someone who'd prided her life on fighting until her last breath, Hatch wondered if it had finally come.

Darkness crept in as the cold water continued its relentless rise. Hatch reached for the opening in a last-ditch effort to pull herself up. Her fingers dug into the dirt and stone. She was losing purchase when two massive hands clamped around her wrists and hauled her body out of the hole.

Raff's strength was shocking, even for a man of his size. He lifted her as easily as he might lift Princess Mayhem, muscles designed for a lifetime of wrestling with eighteen-wheelers and thousand-pound loads making her weight seem negligible. He set her down on solid ground with surprising gentleness.

Hatch collapsed to her hands and knees, coughing up tunnel water that tasted of concrete dust and diesel fuel. Her lungs burned as they expelled the foreign liquid and filled with air that had never tasted so sweet. Rain fell on her back—cold, clean, alive. The most beautiful sensation she'd ever felt.

"Easy there," Raff said, one massive hand patting her shoulder with careful pressure. "You're alright now. All of you."

She looked up through streaming eyes to see the Carter family huddled together beside the Peterbilt, wrapped in emergency blankets that Raff must have pulled from his cab. The truck looked like a mechanical mountain, its chrome exhausts still breathing diesel smoke.

Miles was breathing normally, but his face was pale with shock and exhaustion. Laura held him close, one arm still cradled against her chest, her own eyes wide with shell shock.

Carter watched the smoking ruins of the tunnel with the hollow eyes of a man who'd seen his life's work turned into a weapon, then used to nearly kill everyone he loved most in the world.

"How?" Hatch managed between coughs that brought up more mountain water. "How did you know to come here?"

Raff helped her to her feet, his weathered face creasing with concern. "Heard it on the CB. Tunnel collapse on 214. Chatter said a chopper doing a flyover spotted the mess and called it in, got every driver in earshot buzzing. Figured it'd be a few hours before any real help could get organized—you know how it is with emergency response out here. Multiple jurisdictions, lots of red tape."

He glanced at the devastation, shaking his head at the scope of destruction that had turned a simple mountain highway into a geological crime scene. "I was making my way back from a delivery in Harpers Ferry when I heard the call. Wasn't but twenty minutes out of my way. I pulled the rig onto the wide shoulder just before the tunnel entrance—didn't want to block the road for the crews comin' in."

He gestured toward the ruins with one calloused hand, the gesture taking in tons of rock and twisted metal that had been a functioning tunnel just hours before. "Plus, Princess Mayhem started carrying on something fierce when we got close. Figured if she was worked up, there's probably folks in trouble."

As if summoned by her name, Princess Mayhem appeared in the truck's window, tiny paws pressed against the glass, tail wagging with manic energy. Her bedazzled sweater caught the weak sunlight, throwing tiny rainbows across the cab's interior like a disco ball celebrating their survival.

Hatch looked back at the collapsed tunnel—tons of rock and concrete where a road had been just hours ago. The destruction was complete. David Kern had turned Carter's earthquake prevention technology into an earthquake creation device, then used it to try to erase them from existence.

Hatch looked at the Carter family, alive against all odds. Finally at Raff, this gentle giant who'd appeared exactly when they'd needed him most, like some benevolent deity disguised as a long-haul trucker with a Chihuahua sidekick.

"If it wouldn't be too much trouble," Hatch said, "think we could get a lift out of here?"

Raff's grin could have powered the truck, transforming his weathered features into something that belonged on a greeting card. "Darlin', after what y'all just went through, I'd drive you to the moon if you asked."

They climbed into the cab—the Carter family squeezed into the sleeper berth like refugees from their own lives, Hatch in the passenger seat with Princess Mayhem claiming her lap. The tiny dog turned in three circles and settled down as if this was perfectly normal, as if she hadn't just helped save four lives through the simple expedient of barking at exactly the right moment.

The cab smelled of diesel fuel and honest work, leather seats worn smooth by years of cross-country journeys, air freshener that couldn't quite mask the scent of a man who lived on the road. It was the most welcoming space Hatch had ever occupied.

Raff put the truck in gear and pulled away from the devastation, eighteen wheels rolling toward whatever came next.

THIRTY-TWO

THE PETERBILT ROLLED THROUGH THE VIRGINIA countryside like a gentle giant, its diesel engine purring with the contentment of a machine doing what it was made for. The big rig's eighteen wheels found their rhythm on asphalt still slick from the morning rain, each revolution carrying them farther from the tomb that Hollowback Ridge had nearly become.

Raff kept to the back roads, avoiding the main highways where state police might be converging on the tunnel collapse. These were the routes that truckers knew by heart—ribbons of asphalt that wound through farmland and forest, past weathered barns that had stood since before the interstate system carved its concrete arteries across America. Fields stretched away on either side, still pearled with morning dew that caught the weak sunlight like scattered diamonds.

The landscape felt impossibly peaceful after the violence they'd survived. Cows grazed in pastures bordered by split-rail fences, their bovine indifference to human catastrophe somehow reassuring. A red-tailed hawk circled lazily overhead, riding thermals. This was America as it existed on postcards and in campaign commercials—rolling hills, honest farmland, the kind of pastoral beauty that politicians invoked when they talked about heartland values.

It was also the perfect place to disappear.

Hatch rode shotgun, watching the landscape scroll past through rain-streaked windows that turned the world into an impressionist painting. Every mile between them and Hollowback Ridge felt like a small victory, but she knew they weren't safe. Not yet. Maybe not ever, as long as David Kern drew breath and commanded resources that could turn mountains into murder weapons.

She catalogued the damage from their underground ordeal. Her ankle throbbed with each pulse of her heart, swelling pressing against her boot like a biological vise. Cuts on her hands stung as time washed away the protective coating of adrenaline. Her ribs ached where she'd been slammed against debris during the collapse, each breath a reminder that physics had tried its best to crush them all into paste.

But they were breathing. Heartbeats steady. Minds processing the impossible fact of their survival with the sluggish wonder of people who'd been yanked back from the edge of oblivion.

Behind them in the sleeper berth, the Carter family huddled together under an army surplus wool blanket. The space was cramped—designed for a single trucker grabbing federally mandated rest, rather than a family of refugees from their own lives—but they made it work through the simple expedient of holding each other close.

Miles had claimed Princess Mayhem as his personal therapy dog. The tiny Chihuahua curled on his lap like a furry talisman against the darkness they'd escaped. Her bedazzled sweater—"Bad to the Bone" written in glittery letters that caught the dim light—added an incongruous touch of glamour to their fugitive tableau. The boy's breathing had settled into an easy rhythm, his airways having remembered how to function normally, but his eyes held the glassy look of a child processing trauma in real time.

Laura dozed fitfully, her injured arm cradled against her chest, face pale with the exhaustion from spending the hours prior convinced her family was about to die. Even in sleep, her free hand stayed on Miles' arm, maternal instinct operating on autopilot even when consciousness had temporarily surrendered to exhaustion.

Carter stared out the side window with the hollow eyes of a man watching his world crumble. Every mile that passed beneath their wheels was another mile away from the laboratory where he'd developed technology meant to save lives, another mile deeper into a reality where his life's work had been perverted into an instrument of targeted assassination. His reflection in the glass looked older than it had that morning, aged by the weight of unintended consequences and the terrible mathematics of power corrupted.

They were all in that liminal state between mental and physical exhaustion—too wired to sleep properly, too drained to stay fully alert. The adrenaline crash was hitting hard, leaving them vulnerable and raw, emotions cycling between gratitude for survival and horror at how close they'd come to becoming statistics in David Kern's war against inconvenient truths.

"I need to ask a favor," Hatch said quietly, keeping her voice low enough not to wake the family.

Raff glanced at her. Up close, she could see the network of fine lines around his eyes, likely from decades of squinting into highway glare and reading weather patterns in distant clouds.

"Shoot."

"We need somewhere safe to regroup. Somewhere quiet, off the beaten path. The kind of place that takes cash and doesn't ask questions." Hatch paused, choosing her next words carefully. "But not a dive. These people have been through enough."

She gestured at the sleeping family behind them, noting how Miles' small hand had found its way to Princess Mayhem's collar, his thumb stroking between her neck and ear.

Raff was quiet for a moment. The truck's CB radio crackled with distant chatter—other drivers calling out speed traps, weather conditions, road construction that could cost precious time on delivery schedules. It was the eternal brotherhood of the road sharing information that kept them all moving safely, a network of voices connected by nothing more than radio waves and professional courtesy.

"Handle's Moondog," came a voice through the static. "Got a bear in the bushes at mile marker 847, eastbound. Keep the shiny side up, drivers."

"Thanks for the heads-up, Moondog," Raff replied, keying his mic. "Catch you on the flip."

He set the handset back in its clip and returned his attention to Hatch's request. "Know just the place," he said. "Moonrise Motor Lodge, about forty miles south of here. Run by a fella named Ezra Pike. Used to make the finest white lightning in three counties until the government convinced him there were better ways to make a living."

Hatch cocked an eyebrow in the direction of her oversized chauffeur.

"Now don't get that look," Raff chuckled, the sound warm as summer thunder. "Ezra's straight as an arrow these days. Runs a clean operation—twelve units, all with kitchenettes, cable TV, decent beds. Truckers use it when they need to grab their federally mandated rest periods. Cash only, no questions asked, and Ezra's got a philosophy about people's business being their own."

He downshifted as they approached a grade, the Peterbilt's engine note dropping an octave as it prepared to haul forty tons of truck and trailer up the hill.

"Place is off the interstate grid," he continued. "Known mostly to drivers and the occasional traveling salesman who's learned that sometimes the best accommodations aren't the ones with the biggest signs. Ezra keeps a pot of coffee going twenty-four hours, makes a mean breakfast if you're there at the right time, and has never once asked me where I've been or where I'm going."

"Sounds perfect. If it's not too much trouble—"

Raff cut her off with a wave of his massive hand. "Darlin', after what I just saw back there, ain't nothing too much trouble. Besides, Princess Mayhem's taken a shine to your boy. Look at her."

The radio crackled again. Hatch caught fragments of conversation about the tunnel collapse. State police, emergency services, speculation about what had caused such a catastrophic failure in infrastructure that had stood for seventy years without significant problems. The official story was already taking shape—aging infrastructure, geological instability, a tragic accident that could have happened anywhere in rural America where budget constraints had deferred maintenance for decades.

"Terrible thing," came a voice through the static. "Heard they're still trying to figure out what caused it. Whole damn mountain just came down."

"Freak occurrence," another driver replied. "Read somewhere that these old tunnels weren't built to modern seismic standards. Probably been waiting to fall for years."

Hatch listened to the speculation with the grim satisfaction of someone who knew the truth would never surface in official reports. David Kern had turned Carter's earthquake prevention technology into an earthquake creation device, then used it to try to erase them from existence in a way that left no forensic evidence. The mountain itself had been his murder weapon, geology perverted into an instrument of targeted assassination.

But they were still breathing, still thinking, still capable of bringing him down.

"Saw you leaving the diner," Raff said, his voice carefully neutral. The observation hung in the air like smoke, neither accusation nor curiosity, just a statement of fact.

Hatch tensed, muscles coiling. She'd been wondering when this conversation would come.

"In the backseat of that sedan with the fella who tore out of there like a bat out of hell," he continued, eyes fixed on the road ahead. "Figured there was more to the story than breakfast and conversation."

His tone remained conversational, but there was an undercurrent of something deeper—not suspicion, but a heightened awareness.

"Don't take a genius to connect the dots and see there's more to the story than meets the eye. "

The math was simple enough. Even without knowing the specifics, Raff had pieced together the broad outline of their situation with the instinctive intelligence of someone who'd learned to read the world through observation rather than explanation.

"The less you know," Hatch said quietly, "the better off you'll be."

There were secrets that could kill you just for knowing them. Information that turned innocent people into targets simply by virtue of existing in their heads. Whatever kindness Raff had shown them, whatever decency motivated his actions, she wouldn't repay it by painting a bullseye on his back.

Raff nodded, accepting the boundary she'd drawn with philosophical resignation. "Fair enough. But for what it's worth, you strike me as good people in a bad situation. Sometimes that's all a man needs to know."

His assessment carried the casual authority of someone who'd likely spent years making split-second judgments about strangers—which drivers to trust with convoy information, which hitchhikers were worth the risk, which truck stop conversations were worth joining and which were better avoided. Character was currency, and Raff had clearly decided Hatch and the Carters were worth the investment.

They drove in comfortable silence for a while, the truck eating miles with steady determination. The rain had stopped completely now, leaving the world washed clean and gleaming. Through gaps in the clouds, shafts of sunlight painted the hills in shades of gold and green that belonged on tourism brochures advertising the simple beauty of rural America.

A deer stood at the edge of a meadow, watching their passage with the alert stillness of prey that had learned to recognize the difference between threats and harmless noise. It held its position for a moment, then bounded away.

"You know," Raff said, "I've been driving these roads for fifteen years. Seen all kinds of folks in all kinds of trouble. Most of the time, the ones running are running from something they did. But every now and then, you meet people running from something that was done to them."

He glanced at her meaningfully, eyes holding the kind of understanding that came from a lifetime of watching human nature play out at seventy miles per hour. "Makes a difference in how a man chooses to help."

The observation hit something deep in Hatch's chest, loosening a knot she hadn't realized was there. In a world where trust was a luxury she couldn't afford, where every human connection carried the potential for betrayal or exploitation, Raff's simple decency was a gift she hadn't expected.

Here was a man who'd pulled them from a mountain tomb, asked no questions beyond what was necessary for their safety, and was now offering sanctuary without expectation of explanation or reward. It was the kind of basic human kindness that politicians talked about but rarely demonstrated.

"Get some rest," he said, settling back in his seat. "Papa Bear's got the wheel. Moonrise Motor Lodge is about an hour out, and you look like you could use the downtime."

Hatch didn't argue. There was more coming—she could feel it in her bones, the tension that came before a storm. David Kern wouldn't simply accept their survival. He'd escalate, bring more resources to bear, turn their escape from one trap into the motivation for designing better ones.

But every good soldier knew to steal sleep whenever possible. Rest was ammunition, and she had a feeling she'd need every round.

She closed her eyes and let the Peterbilt's steady rumble carry her toward whatever passed for safety in a world where mountains could be moved by men with the will to bury their enemies alive.

THIRTY-THREE

THE PETERBILT'S AIR BRAKES HISSED AS RAFF BROUGHT the big rig to a gentle stop. Hatch's eyes opened to gray daylight filtering through the cab windows, her internal clock telling her something was different.

"How long was I out?" she asked, stretching muscles that had stiffened during the drive.

"Long enough," Raff said, setting the parking brake. "Figured you needed it more than conversation."

Through the windshield, the Moonrise Motor Lodge spread before them like something from a more innocent time. A hand-painted sign swayed gently in the breeze:

MOONRISE MOTOR LODGE - VACANCY - CLEAN ROOMS, FAIR PRICES

MIND YOUR OWN BUSINESS. AND WE'LL MIND OURS

Below it, in smaller letters that had faded with weather and time:

FORMERLY PIKE'S MOUNTAIN LIGHTNING - EST. 1952.

The main building was a low, rambling structure of local fieldstone and weathered wood, designed to blend into the forested hillside. Twelve units curved around a central courtyard, each with its own parking space and a small porch with rocking chairs. It was the kind of place that existed off the interstate grid, known only to truckers, traveling salesmen, and people who needed to disappear for a while.

The Carter family stirred awake in the sleeper berth. Miles sat up first, blinking at the unfamiliar surroundings. Princess Mayhem stretched and yawned, displaying an impressive set of tiny teeth.

"Where are we?" Laura asked, her voice still thick with exhaustion.

"Somewhere safe," Hatch said, opening her door. "Time to stretch our legs."

"Goodbye, Princess," Miles said, pressing his small hand against the glass. "Thank you for finding us."

Raff leaned over, his weathered face creased with a smile. "Must be you're special, son. Princess Mayhem's particular about her people. Doesn't take to just anybody."

Miles beamed with pride. In the span of a few hours, he'd survived a tunnel collapse and been chosen by a dog wearing a rhinestone collar. For an eight-year-old, it didn't get much better than that.

They climbed down from the cab into air that smelled of pine needles and wood smoke. The rain had stopped, but heavy clouds still pressed low over the mountains, turning the world into shades of gray and green.

Hatch approached the driver's side, extending her hand. "I can't thank you enough, Raff. You saved our lives."

Instead of taking her hand, Raff opened the door and stepped down. He pulled her into a bear hug that lifted her feet off the ground. "I'm a hugger," he said by way of explanation. "Hope you don't mind."

For a moment, Hatch allowed herself to sink into the embrace. Real kindness was stretched thin across the world, but when you found it, you had to breathe it in deep, let it carry you forward to whatever came next.

"Mind?" she said as he set her down. "Hell, I needed that more than I realized."

Raff grinned and climbed back into his cab. "Y'all take care now. And Hatch?" He leaned out the window. "Whatever you're carrying, I got a feeling you're gonna see it through just fine."

The Peterbilt pulled away with a farewell honk of its air horn,

Princess Mayhem visible in the passenger window until the truck disappeared around a bend in the road.

Carter approached as the diesel rumble faded into silence. "Maybe it's best we just give Kern what he wants. I don't think this is a fight we can win." He looked at his family.

"Guys like Kern don't accept surrender. There's only one way to guarantee you and your family's safety. And it has everything to do with bringing to light the dark side of AeroSight."

"If you say so." He let out a low sigh, almost a whimper. "So what's our next move?"

"Yours is to keep your family safe," Hatch said. "The minute Kern learns we're still alive, he'll pull out all the stops. Go scorched earth."

"I still have to deliver the evidence to someone, somewhere," Carter insisted. "That was the whole point—"

"It doesn't have to be you." Hatch had been turning this over in her mind during the drive. "I'll do it. I know the game, know the players. I can get it to the right people."

Carter hesitated, uncertainty flickering across his face. "I don't know. Maybe—"

"Either you trust me or you don't," Hatch said. "No middle ground here."

He studied her face for a long moment, then reached into his jacket and pulled out the thumb drive. The small device looked innocuous in his palm—just plastic and silicon but containing enough information to bring down a man who thought himself untouchable.

"What about us?" he asked as he handed it over. "How will we know if you succeed?"

"If it goes down the way I plan, you'll know." Hatch pocketed the drive, feeling its slight weight like a loaded gun. "Right now, they think we're all dead. That's the only thing keeping it from becoming a reality."

Carter nodded. "And what about you?"

Hatch's smile was sharp as a blade. "Technically, I'm already dead."

She didn't offer any further explanation, and Carter seemed to sense it wasn't the kind of statement that invited questions. Instead, he just nodded again.

"No phones," she continued. "Contact no one. As far as the world knows, the Carter family died in a tunnel collapse in Virginia."

"I really can't thank you enough. My family is alive because of you. I don't know what I would've done if you hadn't come along."

"My goal is to make sure you never have to wonder about that again." Hatch put a hand on the geologist's shoulder. "What you did, deciding to step up when others turned a blind eye, takes an incredible amount of courage. You should be proud of yourself."

"Thank you." His face warmed.

"And now I'm going to see it through."

They walked toward the main building, a structure that managed to be both rustic and welcoming. Through the windows, Hatch could see a small lobby decorated with antique furniture and old photographs of the surrounding mountains.

A bell chimed as they entered, and a man emerged from behind the front desk. Ezra Pike was exactly what central casting would have ordered for a reformed moonshiner—tall and lean, with silver hair and eyes the color of winter sky. His face was creased with the kind of lines that came from decades of outdoor work and honest laughter.

"Was that ole Raff out there?" he asked, glancing toward the parking lot.

"The very one," Hatch confirmed.

Pike gave their bedraggled group a quick once-over. "Looks like you folks need a good shower and some rest," he said. No questions about what had happened or why they were there. Just the practical assessment of a man who'd learned to read people's needs without prying into their business.

Hatch pulled out her wallet from her back pocket. The leather was tacky from the moisture it had absorbed. "These fine people are gonna need a room. Not sure how long. How about I pay for a week up front?"

"My going rate's eighty a night." Pike gave a once-over to the family standing before him. "But you folks look like you could use a break. Forty a night sound fair?"

Hatch nodded. "Do you take cash?"

"My preferred method of payment." Pike dotted his statement with a mischievous wink. "Just need you to fill out this here registration form."

Hatch thumbed the wet bills from her billfold and leaned a little closer, lowering her voice. "How about we bypass the formalities?" She set out the cash on the counter, making sure the proprietor saw the extra bills added.

"Never been much of a fan of paperwork myself."

Pike walked to the lock box attached to the wall behind him and opened it. He retrieved the key for room number seven.

"Wait. You're not staying with us?" Laura looked confused. "What if--" Her voice dropped just above a whisper. "Just what if there's a problem?"

"That's why I've got to go. To see things through. To make sure you don't have anything to worry about again," Hatch said.

Hatch noticed an old Ford F-150 parked beside the office, a hand-written "For Sale" sign taped to the windshield. The truck had seen better decades—rust bloomed along the wheel wells, and the paint had faded to an indeterminate color somewhere between blue and gray.

"How much for the truck?" she asked.

Pike glanced out the window. "Six hundred. Runs good enough, though she's a little ornery. Get you where you're going, provided you ask nice."

"How about five hundred?" Hatch said.

Pike considered this for a moment, then nodded. "I'll give you the discount on account of you being friends with Raff. That man's got good judgment about people."

The transaction complete, Pike handed over two sets of keys—one for the room, one for the truck. Hatch gave the room key to Carter and pocketed the truck key.

They stepped back outside. The gray sky and the ordeals they'd been through made it seem much later than it was. Laura and Miles headed toward their room, exhaustion finally overcoming adrenaline. Carter lingered, studying Hatch with the expression of a man trying to memorize something important.

"You're safe now," she assured him. "Pike's good people, and this place is off the grid. Kern won't find you here."

"What about you?" Carter asked.

“I'll be fine,” Hatch said. "It's Kern who should be worried."

THIRTY-FOUR

THE FORD F-150 GROWLED DOWN THE MOUNTAIN HIGHWAY like an old dog that still had some fight left in it. The steering wheel had a quarter inch of play before the wheels responded, the transmission downshifted with all the subtlety of a freight train, and the radio picked up nothing but static and a lonely country station that seemed to broadcast from another century.

But the engine ran steady, the brakes worked when asked, and the gas gauge held at three-quarters full. Sometimes, reliability mattered more than comfort.

Dusk was settling over the Virginia hills, painting the sky in shades of purple and gold. Hatch kept the truck at a steady sixty-five, just fast enough to make time without attracting attention. The headlights had a slight misalignment that made oncoming traffic flash their high beams in annoyance, but she'd driven worse vehicles under worse conditions.

She pulled out her burner phone and dialed a number she knew by heart.

"Well, well." Banyan's voice came through clear and amused. "Did the information I gave you on the congressman prove useful?"

"It did. But things have escalated." Hatch shifted the phone to her left hand, keeping her right on the wheel as the truck navigated a series of lazy curves. "Remember that favor you thought I was going to ask for eventually?"

"I'm listening."

She gave him the condensed version—Harlan's compromised position, the lie about Carter that had put her exactly where she needed to be, the tunnel collapse, their narrow escape. She kept it clinical, factual, but even the bare bones of the story painted a picture of escalation beyond anything they'd dealt with before.

"Jesus, Hatch. They tried to bury you under a mountain."

"They succeeded. Temporarily." She checked the mirrors, looking for a potential tail and seeing none. "Point is, I'm now in possession of a thumb drive that contains enough evidence to take down AeroSight and hopefully Congressman Harlan in the process."

Banyan was quiet for exactly one beat. "What do you need?"

"Remember the Omnisphere device? Your mobile eavesdropping app?"

"The one that turns smartphones into localized surveillance networks? What about it?"

"I need it deployed in the D.C. area within the next couple hours. Is that possible?"

Banyan's laugh carried the particular satisfaction of a man whose paranoid inventions had just proven their worth. "Funny you should ask. Several three-letter agencies have already bought into the program. It's being field-tested by teams across the eastern seaboard."

"Any of those letters happen to be FBI? Because they're going to want to hear what gets said."

"As a matter of fact, yes. I'll make the call. Tell me where you need coverage, and someone will be listening."

Hatch felt a smile tug at her lips. "As soon as I have the location and time, I'll let you know."

"I'd tell you to be careful, but I know better."

"I passed careful about fifty miles back," Hatch said. "Now I'm heading straight for Oh Shitsville, population me."

"That's my girl. Watch your six out there." The line went dead. Hatch pocketed the phone and focused on the road ahead.

She scrolled through her contacts until she found the number Carter had given her—Ethan Voss's cell phone. The phone that Kern's people had been using to text Carter, pretending to be the dead journalist. The phone that was probably sitting on Kern's desk right now, a trophy from a man who thought he'd eliminated all his problems.

Time to remind him that some problems had a way of digging themselves out of their graves.

She dialed the number and listened to it ring.

Once. Twice. Three times.

On the fourth ring, a voice answered that was smooth as silk and cold as winter steel.

"I was wondering when you'd call," Kern said.

"Been busy."

"I have to admit, I'm impressed. The tunnel collapse should have been quite final. Yet here you are, making social calls from beyond the grave."

"What can I say? I'm hard to kill."

"So it would seem." She could hear him moving, the soft clink of ice in a glass. "Where are you calling from? Somewhere safe, I hope. Because the moment I hang up this phone, every resource at my disposal will be dedicated to finding you and finishing what that mountain started."

"That's assuming you hang up the phone at all."

"And why wouldn't I?"

"Because I have something you want. Something that belonged to Dr. Samuel Carter. Something that could make your life very complicated if it fell into the wrong hands."

The silence stretched for five seconds. Ten. When Kern spoke again, his voice had lost its casual amusement.

"What exactly are you proposing?"

"A trade. The drive for safe passage. You let the Carter family disappear, you call off your dogs, and I hand over the evidence that could destroy everything you've built."

"And if I refuse?"

"Then tomorrow morning, every major news outlet in the country gets a copy of Carter's files. Along with some very compromising photos of Congressman Harlan. Amazing what people will admit to when they think they're in control of the situation."

Another pause. Longer this time.

"You're bluffing."

"Am I? Only one way to find out."

Kern was quiet, calculating odds and outcomes. He spoke again with the tone of a man who'd made his decision.

"Very well. A trade. But it happens on my terms, in a location of my choosing."

"I wouldn't have it any other way."

"The Jefferson Memorial. One hour. Come alone."

"See you there."

Hatch ended the call and dialed Banyan back.

"That was fast," he said.

"Jefferson Memorial. One hour. I need the Omnisphere active and FBI ears on the feed."

"Consider it done." He paused. "For what it's worth, you're either very brave or completely insane."

"Little of both," she said, and ended the call.

THIRTY-FIVE

PARKING IN D.C. WAS LIKE COMBAT—YOU HAD TO BE willing to take risks, adapt to changing conditions, and sometimes settle for positions that weren't ideal but got the job done. Hatch found a spot on East Basin Drive far enough away from the meet location that would provide her time to visually assess her surroundings upon approach.

The walk to the Jefferson Memorial gave her time to catalog her physical inventory. Her ankle throbbed where it had been pinned between the rocks, swelling still straining against her boot. The dried mud from the tunnel painted her clothes in shades of brown and gray, and her hair still carried the grit of pulverized concrete. She caught looks from a few pedestrians, but this was D.C.—a city where the homeless population was staggering and visible desperation drew little more than averted eyes.

She forced herself to walk normally, hiding the slight limp that wanted to favor her injured ankle. Weakness was information, and David Kern was the kind of man who collected information like other people collected stamps.

The memorial rose before her through the evening gloom, its white marble dome and columns glowing under carefully positioned floodlights. The rain had stopped hours ago, but the ground still gleamed with moisture, reflecting the streetlights in fractured patterns that shifted with each passing car. The air carried the clean smell of washed stone and the faint, organic scent of the Tidal Basin after rain.

Hatch approached from the northeast, keeping the memorial steps at her back so she could watch the approaches. A young couple strolled along the water's edge, the woman's laughter carrying across the basin like wind chimes. A maintenance worker in city coveralls moved around the memorial's perimeter, emptying trash cans and picking up the detritus that tourists always left behind. On a bench near the Tidal Basin, a homeless man slept under a collection of newspapers and plastic bags, his shopping cart parked beside him like a faithful dog.

Hatch positioned herself near the memorial's base, where the marble steps met the plaza. From here, she could see the major approach routes while keeping her back to solid stone. The floodlights created pools of brilliant white separated by deep shadows—perfect for concealment, terrible for surveillance.

She checked her phone. Three minutes early. In her experience, punctuality was both a courtesy and a tactical advantage. It let you control the initial positioning, observe the terrain, and watch how your opponent approached.

A jogger passed, earbuds in, breathing steady, paying no attention to anything but the path ahead. A taxi dropped off two tourists who immediately began taking selfies with the memorial as backdrop, their camera flash briefly illuminating the columns like amateur lightning.

No sign of Kern.

The couple by the water had stopped walking and were now standing close together, the man pointing across the basin toward the Washington Monument. The maintenance worker had moved closer, working his way around the memorial's circumference with the methodical patience of a man paid by the hour.

Hatch's ankle pulsed with each heartbeat, a steady reminder of how close she'd come to dying in that tunnel. How close the Carter family had come to disappearing without a trace. How David Kern had been willing to bring down a mountain to bury his problems. Everyone was a potential threat.

Tonight, she'd bury him instead.

8:59 PM.

The tourists finished their photo session and wandered off toward the Metro station, their voices fading into the urban background noise of distant traffic and the occasional horn from the Potomac. The jogger had completed his circuit and disappeared into the darkness beyond the memorial's light.

Then, at exactly 9:00 PM, the shadows between the memorial's columns shifted.

David Kern stepped into the light.

He emerged from the darkness as though born from it—impeccably dressed despite the damp evening, his gray suit unmarked by weather or worry. Behind him, barely visible in the deeper shadows, another figure waited. Larger. Watchful. Ready for violence.

Kern walked with casual confidence like he owned not just the ground he stood on, but everything that happened above it. His shoes—Italian leather, probably worth more than most people's cars—clicked softly against the wet marble as he approached.

He stopped twenty feet away, close enough to speak without raising his voice, far enough to maintain the illusion of safety. His eyes found Hatch and stayed there.

"Ms. Hatch," he said, his voice carrying the same smooth authority from their phone conversation. His gaze swept over her mud-stained clothes, the cuts on her hands. "You look like you've had an interesting evening."

"DAVID," she replied, matching his casual tone. "You look like a man who sleeps well at night."

"Conscience of the righteous. Or the practical. I've found they often amount to the same thing."

The man in the shadows remained still, but Hatch could feel his attention like heat from a fire. Professional. Patient. Waiting for a signal that might never come.

"Shall we get on with this?" Kern asked, clasping his hands behind his back in a gesture that somehow managed to be both relaxed and commanding. "I believe you mentioned a trade."

Hatch smiled. Not far off, the couple lingered. The homeless man on the bench stirred again, and the maintenance worker's movements took on a slightly different rhythm.

"Yes," she said. "Let's talk."

THIRTY-SIX

KERN RAISED HIS LEFT HAND, AND THE FIGURE IN THE shadows stepped forward. The man was built like a linebacker who'd traded his jersey for a tactical vest—thick through the chest and shoulders, with the kind of alert stillness that came from years of standing between bullets and paychecks.

He approached Hatch with a device no bigger than a smartphone, keeping a respectful distance as he walked a slow circle around her. The scanner swept over her body, searching for transmitters, recording devices, weapons—the digital age equivalent of a pat-down.

"She's clean," he reported, stepping back into the shadows with the same fluid efficiency as he'd emerged from them.

Kern nodded, satisfied. "Technology has certainly advanced since the days of having to frisk someone for wires."

"Seems like your tech has also advanced past any legal and ethical boundaries," Hatch replied.

"I see you've still got some fight in you."

"'Til my last breath."

He tilted his head like a man studying an interesting puzzle. "You know, a person with your skill set could be an asset to my organization. Comes with a very nice paycheck too."

"Been there, done that, got the T-shirt." Hatch's voice carried the flat dismissal of someone who'd heard the pitch before. "I'm not here for a job interview."

"Then why are you here? Why go through all this trouble?"

The question hit something deep in Hatch's chest, igniting the cold anger she'd been carrying since Riverton. "Because you launched your little experiment in a town full of good, hardworking people. That trouble you're talking about? That's something you started."

Kern waved a dismissive hand. "What's that saying about war being politics by other means?"

"You attacked civilians on American soil to get your contract pushed through Congress."

"Violence is the best form of leverage." His eyes found the scar that ran along her jaw. "Someone like you should know that all too well. Violence seems etched into the very fabric of your existence."

"After figuring out who you were, I did a little digging into your past, Rachel Hatch." His gaze traveled the length of her visible scars before returning to her face. "You've left a long trail of death and destruction in your wake, both while serving and after. And yet here you are, holding the moral high ground and pointing out the faults in the military-industrial complex."

"I learned along the way that people like you need people like me," Hatch said quietly. "Without us, you run amok and turn small towns into war zones."

"Which brings us to our current situation." Kern's voice took on the patient tone of a professor explaining a simple concept to a slow student. "As you've discovered, I'll go to great lengths to ensure my projects are protected."

"Your project is capable of creating earthquakes. You used it to try to kill an innocent family."

Kern's composure cracked for just an instant, anger flashing across his features like heat lightning. "Where you cry innocent, I see threats to our great country. The problem is you don't see the bigger picture."

"That's because I'm not watching it from a drone camera. I'm on the ground, looking these people in the eyes. Do that enough and you realize that bigger picture isn't the justification you think it is."

Kern shrugged, his mask of control sliding back into place. "I suppose we're not going to see eye to eye on this after all." He straightened his cuffs. "Anyway, you spoke of a trade."

"I give you the evidence on this thumb drive, and you leave Dr. Carter and his family alone. Forever."

"How do I know you don't have copies?"

"You don't." Hatch's honesty was brutal in its simplicity. "But even if I did have a backup, it would never see the light of day—as long as they're safe."

Kern studied her for a moment. "All this for three people you never met before yesterday?”

"Good people deserve protection."

"And what's to stop me from killing you once I have the drive?"

Hatch leveled a stare. "I have my insurance plan too. I disappear, and someone I trust will not only ensure that you get buried, but your partner in crime, Congressman William Harlan gets brought into the spotlight right alongside you."

Kern wasn't shocked by the backup plan—he would have been shocked if she didn't have one. "Leverage is a powerful tool. A fulcrum capable of moving mountains."

"Or bringing them down on your head."

Kern spread his hands in a gesture of finality. "Let's get this over with."

Hatch pulled the thumb drive from her pocket and tossed it through the air. Kern caught it one-handed, his reflexes still sharp despite his expensive lifestyle.

"I'd love to say it was a pleasure doing business with you," he said, pocketing the drive, "but you've proven to be a thorn in my side I'm glad to have removed."

Hatch scanned the memorial grounds, then smiled—a expression that held no warmth whatsoever.

"What are you smiling about?" Kern demanded.

"You know, all technology has its limitations. Like that fancy magic wand your man used to sweep me. Thing is, there's tech out there that can turn this little cellphone in my pocket into an active listening device."

Kern's eyes widened as the implications hit him. "Calhoun!" he called to his bodyguard.

Silence answered him. No movement from the shadows.

His smooth demeanor contorted into something approaching panic as he scanned the memorial grounds. The homeless man was no longer sleeping—he was approaching with the purposeful stride of someone with a job to do. The maintenance worker had abandoned his trash can and was also moving toward them. The romantic couple by the water had separated and were flanking their position from opposite sides.

All of them had FBI badges in their hands. All of them had weapons drawn.

"Funny thing about evidence," Hatch said as Kern found himself surrounded. "You're holding the original, right there in your pocket. Thanks for the confession, by the way. Treason isn't something the federal justice system looks upon favorably."

"You—" Kern started, but the lead agent, the man who'd been playing homeless, cut him off.

"David Kern, you're under arrest for conspiracy against the United States, terrorism, and about twelve other federal charges that are going to put you away for several lifetimes."

THIRTY-SEVEN

THE AGENT MOVED IN WITH PRACTICED EFFICIENCY, grabbing Kern's left wrist and clicking the first cuff into place with the mechanical precision of someone who'd done this a thousand times. But as the second cuff swung toward his right wrist, Kern's body exploded into motion.

Years of special forces training overrode the shock of capture. He pivoted hard on his right foot, using the agent's forward momentum against him, wrenching the man off balance. The open cuff became a weapon as Kern hooked it against the agent's throat, the steel pressing into the carotid artery with enough pressure to draw a thin line of blood.

"Step back!" Kern commanded, backpedaling with the agent held against his chest as a human shield. "All of you!"

The other agents raised their weapons instantly, muzzles tracking but unable to find a clean shot. Training warred with desperation—they had a federal agent's life in the balance and a target who knew exactly how to exploit that fact.

Hatch moved with fluid precision, staying in step with Kern's retreat, maintaining actionable distance without triggering his panic response. Close enough to act, far enough to avoid spooking him into killing his hostage.

"There's nowhere you can run," she said, voice calm but carrying an edge of finality. "No escaping this."

Kern's eyes found hers over the agent's shoulder. His mouth curved into something that might have been a smile if it had contained any warmth. "I don't know about that. I hear there are some beautiful places with non-extradition treaties. Costa Rica has lovely beaches this time of year."

He kept backpedaling, scanning the memorial grounds for escape routes, his expensive Italian leather shoes clicking against the wet marble with each careful step. The kind of footwear designed for boardrooms and five-star restaurants, not tactical situations on rain-slicked stone.

His heel caught the edge of a crack in the walkway—just a hairline fracture in the memorial's foundation, invisible until it mattered. The leather sole, smooth from indoor wear, betrayed him completely. His foot slipped sideways with the kind of inevitable physics that no amount of training could overcome.

The stumble loosened his grip for exactly one heartbeat. The agent twisted free, rolling away from his captor with the desperate energy of someone who'd just felt death's breath on his neck.

Hatch pounced.

She hit Kern low and hard, driving her shoulder into his center mass as he fought to regain his balance. They crashed to the marble with bone-jarring impact. Hatch was prepared for the impact and immediately fought for position, taking the mount and trying to control his hips and limit his options.

Kern wasn't finished and launched a counter by shifting his body sideways. In a deft move born of training and experience, he swept her legs and was now on top, bearing his weight down on her. The open cuff was still locked to his left wrist, and he swung it like a hooked blade, the steel edge whistling past Hatch's face close enough to part her hair. The second pass caught her across the left cheek, opening a line of fire from her jaw to her temple. Blood welled instantly, warm against the cold night air.

She gritted her teeth and pressed forward, using the pain as fuel rather than distraction. This was familiar ground, the close-quarters violence where size mattered less than technique and determination mattered most of all. She locked her legs tight around his midsection and arched her back, creating some distance between herself and the improvised weapon.

Kern pressed his weight down on her and swung the cuff in a desperate attempt to lacerate her throat.

Kern ignored the commands of the officers to drop the weapon. But the circle of armed FBI agents served as a momentary distraction.

She could see the rage in his eyes. But anger clouds judgement. And in it, opportunity presented. Hatch released her right leg from his waist and swung it around, threading it across his neck and catching his extended arm, the one wielding the cuff, and pulled him into the triangle choke. Her ankles locked behind his head, creating a vice that physics made inescapable.

"Let it go," she commanded, applying pressure to his elbow joint, bending it against its natural range of motion. The pain delivered was etched into his face, forcing his fingers to spasm open. The weaponized end clattered to the marble while the cuff itself remained attached to his wrist.

Kern's eyes bulged as the choke tightened. She felt his energy dissipate. Weakened, Hatch rolled him off while maintaining the hold. As she righted herself, adding her body weight to the pressure, Kern let out a rasp. He thrashed, trying to power out of the hold, but Hatch rode his movements like a sailor in a storm, maintaining position through balance and leverage rather than strength.

His face darkened from red to purple, oxygen debt mounting with each failed attempt to escape. She reached down and pulled his head, further tightening the vice. From this position, one hard twist of her hips would finish the job and send Kern to a well-deserved hell of his own making. She was in control of his fate. Life or death were a matter of choice. Hatch made hers.

Finally, his struggles weakened, then stopped entirely. His body went limp, unconscious but breathing. Hatch released the hold and rolled clear, breathing hard, blood from her cheek dripping onto the memorial's white marble.

FBI agents swarmed in immediately, hauling Kern's unconscious form upright and securing him with proper restraints this time. His hands cuffed behind his back, legs shackled, the full federal treatment for someone who'd just assaulted a federal officer.

The lead agent approached, touching his throat where the cuff had drawn blood, his expression holding the particular respect of someone who'd just been saved by superior technique.

"Hell of a takedown," he said simply.

Hatch wiped blood from her cheek with the back of her hand, the cut already slowing its bleeding. "He's all yours now."

As they loaded Kern's unconscious body into the back of an unmarked sedan, his eyes fluttered open just long enough to meet hers through the window. Even semiconscious, the fury was unmistakable. The rage of someone who'd never been outfought, never been humbled, never been reduced to just another criminal in the back of a government vehicle.

"This isn't over," he mouthed through the glass.

Hatch touched her bleeding cheek and smiled. "Yeah, it is."

The sedan pulled away into the D.C. night, carrying David Kern toward a federal holding facility where his expensive suits wouldn't matter, where his connections couldn't reach, where his only company would be the concrete walls and steel bars that democracy used to cage its monsters.

The lead agent continued as the taillights disappeared into traffic, his weathered face holding genuine respect mixed with professional concern. "Your friend briefed us on the situation," he said, referring to Banyan. "Got us up to speed on what we were walking into. This country owes you a debt of gratitude."

"I prefer my name stays out of any reports."

"Your friend said you'd say that too." The agent's smile held the particular warmth of someone who understood that some heroes preferred shadows to spotlights. "What about the Carter family?"

"They're at the Moonrise Motor Lodge, about forty miles south of the tunnel collapse. Run by a man named Ezra Pike."

"We'll contact the state police and have them head over to keep watch until we have a protection detail there to take over." He paused, studying her face with the expression of someone trying to memorize details for a report that would be classified above his clearance level. "If we need to reach you?"

"You won't be able to."

"Where are you heading now?"

Hatch looked out across to where the lights of the Washington Monument reflected in the dark water like fallen stars. The cut on her cheek had stopped bleeding, leaving only a thin line that would heal into another small scar to add to her collection.

"The intersection of everywhere and nowhere," she said. "But I've got a birthday party to attend first."

THIRTY-EIGHT

HATCH DROVE WEST, ENSURING HER JOURNEY TOOK A deliberate detour around any tunnels. No need to test the fates so soon after Hollowback Ridge had tried to make her a permanent resident. She'd slept the sleep of the dead at a roadside motel in a small town outside Pittsburgh, where the desk clerk took cash without questions and the room key was actual metal attached to a plastic tag shaped like the Liberty Bell.

Feeling refreshed and recharged for the first time in weeks, she set out for Colorado with the kind of unhurried purpose that came from having nowhere urgent to be and no one shooting at her. Hatch had timed her journey so she could stretch out the days without pushing the limits of Pike's beat-up old Ford, letting the miles unspool at their own pace through America's heartland.

The radio played in the background, a soundtrack to the endless ribbon of asphalt that connected everywhere to somewhere else. A country song about redemption wound down, the singer's gravelly voice carrying the weight of hard-learned lessons.

The song faded as steel guitar gave way to the DJ's voice, warm and familiar as an old friend calling from across the miles. "That was Jake Morrison with 'Stand Your Ground,' climbing the charts faster than a squirrel up a pecan tree. Beautiful morning out there, folks—calling for bright skies and spring-like conditions across the tri-state area. Perfect day for a drive with the windows down."

His tone shifted to that particular cadence radio personalities used when they were about to deliver news that would make people sit up and pay attention. "Speaking of making headlines, we've got some breaking news that's got Washington buzzing like a kicked hornet's nest. The CEO of AeroSight Defense Systems was arrested yesterday on charges of conspiracy, terrorism, and—get this—treason. And if that wasn't enough drama for your Monday morning coffee, charges have also been filed against Congressman William Harlan for his role in the whole mess."

The DJ's chuckle carried a note of salacious gossip that belonged in barbershops and beauty salons rather than federal courtrooms. "Now, I'm not one to kick a man when he's down, but apparently this distinguished member of Congress has some interesting hobbies that are making the rounds on social media. Let's just say the photos involve handcuffs, but not the kind you'd expect in a law-and-order campaign ad. Not sure what his wife's gonna have to say about that little revelation."

Hatch clicked the radio off with more force than necessary, cutting the DJ's commentary mid-sentence. Some victories were better savored in silence.

Her phone rang, the sound sharp in the sudden quiet of the cab. She glanced at the display and couldn't suppress a small smile.

"Did you hear the news?" Banyan asked, his voice barely containing the glee.

"Can't thank you enough for having my back on this one."

"On what one?" The innocence in his voice was about as convincing as a three-dollar bill, but she could hear his smile through the connection.

"I've got one last favor to ask."

He let out an exaggerated sigh that managed to convey both resignation and affection. "Go ahead. "

"My Jeep is buried under forty feet of rock and timber somewhere near Hollowback Ridge. Eventually they'll dig it out—probably take them weeks to clear all that debris. There's a gun in a hidden compartment behind the rear wheel well." She paused, watching a hawk circle lazily over a field of winter wheat that was just beginning to show green. "Probably best if that particular piece of evidence never finds its way into an investigator's hands."

"Consider it done."

"Don't worry. I won't be asking for any more favors after this." Hatch let the words hang in the air for a moment, weighted with the kind of finality that came from decisions made in the dark hours before dawn. "I don't have many friends in this world, Banyan. The ones I do have, I try not to burn."

"Ditto." He let a moment pass, filled only by the sound of tires on asphalt and the distant hum of the Ford's aging engine. "Don't take this the wrong way, but I hope the next time I hear from you is just to say hello. Maybe to tell me about some boring civilian problem like your neighbor's dog barking too much or your cable going out during the big game."

"Me too."

"Seriously though, Hatch. Every gunslinger has to hang up their guns at some point. If they don't, they're likely to have them hung up for them—permanently." He let the weight of his words settle. "It's a hard truth of the world you and I live in. The house always wins eventually, unless you're smart enough to walk away while you're still breathing."

Hatch had been giving serious thought to exactly that question during the long hours of driving through Pennsylvania farmland and Ohio river valleys.

How many dances with death until the music stopped playing? How many times could you roll the dice before they came up snake eyes?

She looked out at the open road stretching toward the horizon, where the morning sun painted everything in shades of gold. Somewhere ahead lay Colorado, her niece's birthday party, and the promise of a life that didn't require looking over her shoulder.

"Well, I'm heading for normal," she said finally. "Maybe this time it'll take."

"I hope so. You've earned it, if anyone has."

"You take care of yourself, Banyan."

"Fair winds and following seas, my friend."

The line went dead, leaving only the steady hum of the engine and the whisper of wind through the truck's weatherstripping. Hatch thought about calling her mother to let her know she was on her way, maybe give her an estimated arrival time so she could prepare for the chaos that seemed to follow in her daughter's wake.

But if Hatch had learned anything from her years of dancing on the edge of violence, it was that surprises kept life interesting. Sometimes the best gift you could give someone was simply showing up when they needed you most.

The road stretched ahead, empty and full of promise, carrying her toward whatever came next. In the rearview mirror, the shadows of her past grew smaller with each passing mile, finally small enough to fit in the space between memory and forgetting.

For the first time in longer than she could remember, Rachel Hatch was driving toward something instead of running from it.

And that, she reflected as the Ford carried her west toward home, was a hell of a good feeling.

THE RACHEL HATCH SERIES

Drift

Downburst

Fever Burn

Smoke Signal

Firewalk

Whitewater

Aftershock

Whirlwind

Tsunami

Fastrope

Sidewinder

Redaction

Mirage

Faultline

Switchback

RACHEL HATCH SHORT STORIES

Fractured

Proving Ground

The Gauntlet

Ricochet

Join the LT Ryan reader family & receive a free copy of the Rachel Hatch story, Fractured. Click the link below to get started:

https://ltryan.com/rachel-hatch-newsletter-signup-1

ALSO BY L.T. RYAN

Find All of L.T. Ryan's Books on Amazon Today!

<u>The Jack Noble Series</u>

The Recruit (free)

The First Deception (Prequel 1)

Noble Beginnings

A Deadly Distance

Ripple Effect (Bear Logan)

Thin Line

Noble Intentions

When Dead in Greece

Noble Retribution

Noble Betrayal

Never Go Home

Beyond Betrayal (Clarissa Abbot)

Noble Judgment

Never Cry Mercy

Deadline

End Game

Noble Ultimatum

Noble Legend

Noble Revenge

Never Look Back

Bear Logan Series

Ripple Effect

Blowback

Take Down

Deep State

Bear & Mandy Logan Series

Close to Home

Under the Surface

The Last Stop

Over the Edge

Between the Lies

Caught in the Web

The Marked Daughter

Beneath the Frozen Sky

Rachel Hatch Series

Drift

Downburst

Fever Burn

Smoke Signal

Firewalk

Whitewater

Aftershock

Whirlwind

Tsunami

Fastrope

Sidewinder

Redaction

Mirage

Faultline

Switchback

Mitch Tanner Series

The Depth of Darkness

Into The Darkness

Deliver Us From Darkness

Cassie Quinn Series

Path of Bones

Whisper of Bones

Symphony of Bones

Etched in Shadow

Concealed in Shadow

Betrayed in Shadow

Born from Ashes

Return to Ashes

Risen from Ashes

Into the Light

Blake Brier Series

Unmasked

Unleashed

Uncharted

Drawpoint

Contrail

Detachment

Clear

Quarry

Dalton Savage Series

Savage Grounds

Scorched Earth

Cold Sky

The Frost Killer

Crimson Moon

Dust Devil

Savage Season

Maddie Castle Series

The Handler

Tracking Justice

Hunting Grounds

Vanished Trails

Smoldering Lies

Field of Bones

Beneath the Grove

Disappearing Act

Affliction Z Series

Affliction Z: Patient Zero

Affliction Z: Abandoned Hope

Affliction Z: Descended in Blood

Affliction Z : Fractured Part 1

Affliction Z: Fractured Part 2 (Coming Soon)

Alex Hayes Series

Trial By Fire (Prequel)

Fractured Verdict

11th Hour Witness

Buried Testimony

The Bishop's Recusal

The Silent Gavel

Stella LaRosa Series

Black Rose

Red Ink

Black Gold

White Lies

Silver Bullet

Avril Dahl Series

Cold Reckoning

Cold Legacy

Cold Mercy

Savannah Shadows Series

Echoes of Guilt

The Silence Before

Dead Air

Receive a free copy of The Recruit. Visit:

https://ltryan.com/jack-noble-newsletter-signup-1

ABOUT THE AUTHORS

L.T. RYAN is a *Wall Street Journal* and *USA Today* bestselling author, renowned for crafting pulse-pounding thrillers that keep readers on the edge of their seats. Known for creating gripping, character-driven stories, Ryan is the author of the *Jack Noble* series, the *Rachel Hatch* series, and more. With a knack for blending action, intrigue, and emotional depth, Ryan's books have captivated millions of fans worldwide.

Whether it's the shadowy world of covert operatives or the relentless pursuit of justice, Ryan's stories feature unforgettable characters and high-stakes plots that resonate with fans of Lee Child, Robert Ludlum, and Michael Connelly.

When not writing, Ryan enjoys crafting new ideas with coauthors, running a thriving publishing company, and connecting with readers. Discover the next story that will keep you turning pages late into the night.

Connect with L.T. Ryan
Sign up for his newsletter to hear the latest goings on and receive some free content
➜ https://ltryan.com/jack-noble-newsletter-signup-1

Join the private readers' group
➜ https://www.facebook.com/groups/1727449564174357

Instagram ➜ @ltryanauthor
Visit the website ➜ https://ltryan.com
Send an email ➜ contact@ltryan.com

Printed in Dunstable, United Kingdom

71356241R00137